The McKinnon
The Beginning

Book One
Part 1
The McKinnon Legends
A Time Travel Series

Ranay James

Ranay James
1209 South Main Street
#126
Lindale, Texas 75771
www.ranayjames.com

Publishers Note: This is a work of fiction. Names, characters, places, and incidents are a product of the author's imagination. Locales and public names are sometimes used for atmospheric purposes. Any resemblance to actual people, living or dead, or to businesses, companies, events, institutions, or locales is completely coincidental.

The McKinnon The Beginning Book One Part 1 of The McKinnon Legends A Time Travel Series — 1st ed.
ISBN 978-0-9967862-4-9

Other Series By Ranay James

Series by Ranay James available in e-book format at all
major retailers through the following website:

WWW.booklaunch.io/ranayjames

The McKinnon Legends A Time Travel Series
The McKinnon American Men A Romantic Suspense Series
Vampires Of Nirvana is a ten part series that with each
book will leave you begging for more. If you love the
McKinnons, then you are going to love the royal family of
Nirvana.

Print Editions Available:

Vampires of Nirvana:Book 1- Never Kiss Me Goodbye
Vampires of Nirvana: Book 2 - Point of No Return
The McKinnon The Beginning: Book One Part 1
The McKinnon The Beginning: Book One Part 2
Unfinished Business: Book Two Part 1
Unfinished Business: Book Two Part 2

Large Print Editions:
The McKinnon The Beginning: Book One Part 1
Vampires of Nirvana Book 1 - Never Kiss Me Goodbye

Audiobook Editions:
**Audiobooks available at Audiobooks.com and
Audible.com**

To my husband—thank you for being my partner through life and supporting my dreams.

I have been impressed with the urgency of doing. Knowing is not enough; we must apply. Being willing is not enough; we must do.
—LEONARDO DA VINCI

Chapter 1

Elderage Castle, England
Christmas Eve
1486

"Wake, child! Run! Run, Morgan, go!"
Morgan heard the frantic voice yanking her as if by a
physical force from a deep and dreamless sleep. Already
the fire was spreading at an alarming speed, and toxic black
smoke was so thick that she could hardly see the hand in
front of her face. She labored just to breathe as the fingers
of death reached for her, wrapping around her legs in a
certain death grip.

"Run!" She heard the voice again.

"Mamma! Da!" she screamed as the ceiling began to
collapse around her. "John? James? Rhiannon?" She called
for her siblings as she crawled along the stone floor. They
had been sleeping in the same bed with her yet now were
nowhere that she could see. The flames were gaining
ground, licking at her gown, and embers singed her hair as
she found the chamber door.

"Turn right, Morgan, and run as fast as you can."
She unflinchingly followed her mother's voice.

Morgan ran down the hallway, then traversed the stone
stairs. The heat was so intense that the stone burned the
tender skin on the bottom of her feet, yet she was heedless
of the pain.

"Turn left, now!" her mother's voice demanded of her.

Morgan instantly obeyed, finding herself only a few
feet from the main entry door. Flames completely engulfed
the opening in a deadly inferno of burning wood and
molten metal.

"Trust me, child. Go through that door." Morgan felt, rather than heard, the voice in her head.

Morgan's sense of survival was almost too strong to follow her mother's demand.

"Trust me, go! There will be a way provided. Go or die!"

Morgan took a leap of faith. Bounding over the last three steps of the staircase, she made a dash for that flaming door. Only feet from the massive blaze, the door barring her exit fell, crashing outward as a massive timber fell from the ceiling. This unburned beam was the bridge she needed to escape through the gap left by the missing entryway.

Out into the night, Morgan ran on bare feet until she could no longer feel the searing heat. Turning to look back, she called to her family and screamed at the top of her lungs, forcing her voice to rise above the roar of the firestorm.

Had her family survived? She saw no one in the outer bailey as she ran through the outer gates, trying to escape the fire that was rapidly spreading to all the outbuildings and stables. It was as if the whole of the castle was deserted and she was the only living soul.

She saw her father stumble out of the castle carrying her mother, and relief flooded through her. She ran to him where he had fallen, burned and dying.

"Mamma, Da! Oh God, somebody help them!" she cried, looking around for any hope of assistance for the father she adored and the mother she loved beyond life itself. There was no help for either of them as she watched her adored father take his last breath holding his beloved duchess, whom he had died to save.

His efforts had been in vain.

Alison Pembridge, Sixth Duchess of Seabridge, fought the hands of death pulling her into the spirit world. She had one thing she had to do before leaving this physical earth behind her.

"Morgan, listen to me." Alison struggled to speak past the pain and damage to her lungs from the searing flames. "I love you, heart of my heart."

"Mamma, save your strength. You'll be fine. I'll make you better, I promise. Just don't die, please. I'll take good care of you."

Morgan's young mind couldn't fathom what was actually happening. Her brain wasn't allowing her to see this for what it was. Alison knew that. Reality would find her lovely daughter soon enough.

Alison had foreseen this night long before she had married the dashing and charismatic Morgan James Pembridge, Sixth Duke of Seabridge. She couldn't change things or stop the hands of fate. She had tried to spare her children the pain of what this night had brought to them all. As a mother, she had failed. Destiny had brought them here, regardless of her efforts to change the flow of time and how this event would unfold. It simply had been out of her control.

She had also foreseen other events, and she had to pass on to her daughter what she could while there was still time.

"Listen to me, child. You must be strong. You're now the Seventh Duchess of Seabridge. It's your destiny, and the path ahead will make you strong if you don't let it kill you. Only you can find the inner strength to survive, Morgan. Take heart, the great sorrow will pass and great triumph will follow. Remember the contract I showed you?"

Morgan nodded as tears streamed, cutting a clear path down her soot-covered face.

"Don't forget it, Morgan, and just as you heard my voice tonight, know I will always be there to guide you in times of greatest crisis. I... love... you." Alison's hand fell away from her daughter's face.

"Mamma? Mamma!" Thirteen-year-old Morgan watched as the light went out of her mother's emerald green eyes.

Morgan screamed as her uncle Lester Brentwood picked her up and carried her away from her parents' bodies.

"Nay! Put me down! Let me go!"

She fought him as she saw a man dragging her father farther from the flames.

Lester needed indisputable proof his stepbrother, sister in law, and the children were dead.

"Morgan, listen to me. They're gone! They're all gone except you and me." Lester watched as Elderage, his ancestral home, went up in flames. "I'm taking you back to Seabridge. Then I'll go to King Henry. As your father's only brother, I'm your only living relative, Morgan. You're now my responsibility."

Morgan was numb and too distraught to notice that a wagon, a covered carriage, and several horses were already ready to leave. She had suffered the greatest loss a child could experience, but she clung to her mother's words. "*I will guide you in times of crisis.*"

Morgan could feel her mother near as she folded herself up into a ball on the uncomfortable seat of that carriage and allowed her mind to go blank.

This would be the first of many times in the next seven years she would retreat into herself out of self-preservation.

To survive, one does what one has to.

For Morgan it was to become a way of life.

Chapter 2

Seabridge Castle
England
Spring 1493

It had been over seven years since that fateful Christmas
Eve. Morgan, now a young woman of twenty, stood, taking
a deep breath for courage.
"You can do this," Morgan whispered, her words
disappearing into the darkness of the secret passageway.
"You must do this, my child." Her mother's voice
came back, echoing softly on the drafty air.
In spite of the damp and chill lingering in the midnight
air, Morgan found herself wiping away a bead of sweat
inching its way down her temple. Escape was her focus,
and having planned this moment of escape for years, she
knew with utter certainty it was now or never. She wasn't
about to let a little thing like fear keep her from obtaining
the one thing she hadn't had in seven years.
Freedom.
She could smell freedom. She tasted it on the stale
salty air as it bubbled up from the depths of the castle.
Her uncle had indeed returned her to Seabridge after
the death of her family; however, he had seen that she
remained locked away here, neglected and abused. His
subjects were too afraid of him to help her. Morgan was
held captive in the castle, simply too isolated for anyone to
even realize she was a prisoner in her own home, beaten,
starved, and alone in her torment.
"You can do this, heart of my heart." The soft
encouragement of her mother's ghost answered her
trepidation. She closed her eyes against the blackness that
would lead her to the damp bowels of the castle. Plunging

through the secret door of the tower room, Morgan quickly felt for the lever.

By fortune she had found the doorway five years earlier.

Morgan remembered the day clearly:

Desperate for warmth, Morgan pulled the tapestry off the wall and wrapped it around herself.

Huddled and shivering against the opposite wall, she stared, transfixed, for days on end. Then, as if by magic... One moment she was looking at bare stone and the next she saw it: gaps in the mortar that were too regular to be caused by age alone. She sprang to her feet, flinging the moldy tapestry behind her. Hope spurred her to push and prod and smooth her hand across the rough-hewn surface, searching for the key to open this hidden door. The heady promise of freedom sharpened her focus, and it wasn't long before she found a loose chunk of mortar that, when lifted, let the door swing inward.

That black maw had terrified her, and she quickly closed the door again, hanging the tapestry back in its place lest someone else discover the secret.

She had never taken it down, no matter how cold she had felt.

In the years following that grand discovery, Morgan's sheer willpower and determination fueled her exploration of the narrow passageway that some long ago ancestor had been insightful enough to build. Had she been a man, she would have had to turn sideways to traverse the path. Over time her courage grew as the cobwebs cleared, and remains of long-dead rodents were crushed beneath her feet. Finding other entrances, she began raiding other rooms for items she thought would help when she finally made her bid to escape. She kept them hidden in a stolen sack just inside the passageway of her cell.

Picking up the sack of items she had managed to collect on her nightly excursions, she dug through them to find trousers, a shirt, and a knife, which she placed soundlessly on the floor of the passage. Slipping off the ragged dress, Morgan quickly used the scraps as undergarments to bind her breasts. Then she pulled on one of the two sets of stolen clothing. With no one to care or help to tend her needs, there had been no opportunity for a haircut. In seven years her hair had grown past her waist. She knew it had to go. It was crucial to her disguise as a stable boy.

She awkwardly sawed across the long braid where it was gathered at the base of her neck until the last of the strands broke free. The weight of it transferring from her head to her hand felt like a different kind of freedom.

Placing the severed tresses into a second sack once used for seed, she prayed the confinement would keep any of the long dark strands from inadvertently making their way under the opening and giving away the existence of the door. If she had to abort this escape attempt, she needed to ensure her secret was safe. Not that she would have a reasonable explanation for how she cut her hair without a proper tool, should she have to return unsuccessfully in this attempt. Tying a knot in the top of the sack, she placed it to the side, leaving it behind along with any remaining self-doubt.

From this point to the next, Morgan would be in complete darkness, knowing that each of the chambers had slits in the walls for secret viewing. She couldn't risk someone seeing a light source shining through the walls, alerting someone to her presence.

It's neither here nor there, she thought. She didn't need the light, knowing every passageway as intimately as she did.

When she began to venture out over five years ago, there had been several narrow escapes. Almost immediately, tales began to circulate of certain parts of the

7

castle being haunted with the spirit of her long-dead mother. A few servants came forward claiming to have seen the ghost of the Sixth Duchess wandering the castle at night, searching for her dead children. Some had gone as far as to say the duchess had spoken to them through the walls.

Her uncle had dismissed all this as the ranting of the ignorant. Morgan had taken full advantage. Knowing none of the superstitious folk would venture to the places they thought to be haunted bought her time to roam the castle more freely. Morgan smiled, the thought giving her courage. The only thing wandering the corridors of Seabridge was her, and she had no intentions of dying anytime soon.

She moved slowly, feeling her way along the passage, careful not to give her presence away to the occupants in the chambers just inches away. Step by agonizing step, Morgan kept her breathing even and silent just as she had practiced.

Inching her way closer to her first destination, Morgan felt for the latch located at the top of the door. This passage exited into the solar, opening less than two feet from the desk that had once belonged to her father.

Stopping at the panel, which, to the unknowing eye, looked like the third in a trio of bookcases lining the wall behind the desk, she placed her ear to the cool surface to listen for evidence of anyone in the chamber. With her uncle still in London for the Easter celebration, she doubted there was any activity in this part of the castle, especially at this hour. Yet caution was still the rule. She hadn't survived this long by being reckless.

Silently, the latch released, and, holding the panel from springing open, she cracked it ever so slightly. Peering through the crack in the panel, Morgan could see there was no one in the solar. Breathing a sigh of relief, she slipped through the opening.

Crouching down behind the desk, she silently closed the bookcase behind her, gently placing pressure until hearing the soft click of the latch. In the silence of the night it sounded very loud, yet no one came to investigate. She had cleared another hurdle.

The second escape hatch was a scuttle hole low on the wall in the opposite corner, which opened out to a landing for a set of very narrow stairs leading down into the maze of tunnels beneath the castle. Feeling along the wall for the edge she knew was there, Morgan pressed another stone designed to move with ease. Again, an engineering wonder that a massive stone could be moved by a slip of a woman. She looked around the darkened room for what she hoped was the last and final time.

This was the same room she had once played chess in with her father. That wonderful time seemed ages ago, before the fire consumed her family at her uncle's estate, leaving her sole heir to the family fortune, the dukedom called Seabridge. She had become the Seventh Duchess that fateful night which claimed the lives of her father, mother, twin sister, and brothers. In a flash, she had become the ward of her father's stepbrother, her only known living relation.

The man was evil, and over the seven years that she had been under his care, he had placed his share of emotional and physical scars upon her. With good reason, she had grown to suspect he had killed her family for his own personal gain. If she stayed, Morgan knew he would eventually kill her too.

"No more. It ends tonight," she vowed as she stared into the void left by the stone. Morgan inhaled the stale, cold air bubbling up from the frigid depths of the castle. She knew it was the smell of liberty.

Morgan stared into the darkness. Only three hundred yards of underground tunnel separated her from the edge of the paddocks and her means of escape. She had spent years exploring the miles of tunnels, hoping she would find the one tunnel that opened past the castle walls. After years of searching, she had been victorious, not only in finding the bolt hole, but also in finding the contract between her father and the king.

And none too soon, Morgan thought.

She was aware King Henry had refused Lester's petition to marry her the previous summer. Lester unsuccessfully argued there was no blood relation between them. Her grandfather's second wife was Lester's mother, and he was ten years old when they married. It had not mattered to the king. Henry really didn't care if her father and Lester had shared neither the same father nor mother. Lester wasn't of noble blood. His mother only married into it. Morgan, by contrast, was a not so distant relative to the king and royal family. The king had given her uncle a royal "Nay!" and sent him packing. She overheard some of the house servants laughing at his ousting by the king, feeling it was less than he actually deserved. Morgan agreed.

At the time, her triumph had been very short-lived.

Lester must have vowed that if he couldn't marry her to secure the dukedom and titles for himself, he would marry her to someone he could control. Consequently, he had paraded her in front of a score of potential husbands as if she were a piece of property to go to the highest bidder.

She remembered hearing about spinster relatives, who were considered eccentric and had lived respectable lives courtesy of their wealth and intelligence. Morgan knew she had no use for marriage; she was almost past a respectable marriageable age, and she was more than capable of making her own decisions about her life. She had had nothing but time to plan her future. If she could only survive another couple of weeks until her twenty-first birthday, she would then be truly free. She would never to have to answer to any man except for the king himself.

After years of searching through the cracks and crevices of the castle, she had finally found the contract her father had drawn up between King Henry and himself when she was a child. Her mother had shown it to her only days before the fire, reading it to her and explaining paragraph by paragraph how the agreement worked.

She remembered the day clearly…

"Morgan, your father and I love you, and as our first born, we have discussed your future at great length. He and I are in agreement that your happiness is the most important thing for us. It is important for all our children."

"I am happy."

Morgan remembered feeling content at that moment sitting by the large window in her father's solar with her sister sitting next to her reading one of the valuable books her father had in his prized collection. Her beautiful mother was sitting only a few feet from them with the folds of her skirt spread out around her as she sat in the cushioned chair next to the fireplace.

Lady Pembridge patted the seat next to her. "Come here, my sweet girls." She had waited for Morgan and Rhiannon to join her. Morgan sat at her mother's right and Rhiannon situated herself on a cushion on the floor by her feet. "Morgan, you are our eldest child and should the unthinkable happen, your father and I wanted to be sure that all of you were taken care of properly. Not that I'm saying anything will happen, it is wise to have a plan in place."

"What plan, mamma?" Rhiannon asked. She was so quiet and she rarely spoke. As a twin, Rhiannon and Morgan could communicate without words and often did. Her vocalizing the question confirmed to Morgan that Rhiannon was engaged in the conversation and not lost in her own magical world of make-believe. It was rare that anything would pull her out of her daydreams. The older they became the more Rhiannon withdrew.

"Well, girls, not every man is as good and decent as your father," Lady Pembridge stated. "Life for a woman can be hard. This is especially true if the circumstances are not, shall I dare say, ideal. Because of that your father and I want you to have some leverage. We want you to have the ability of input into your circumstances. I want to read you something and it is very important that you understand what this document represents."

Morgan sat beside her mother and peered at the parchment that contained several wax seals. One belonged to the king.

"Now, girls, this document is an agreement between your father and the king. The decree states clearly that should either of you find yourself in the hands of a guardian and not find a husband of your own choosing— and that is the key to this whole thing: a husband of your own choice—then on your twenty-first birthday your inheritance is yours to manage as you see fit, without any outside interference. Morgan, Seabridge is yours as you are our first born. I don't care that the archaic practice is only boys being in line to inherit. It's simply offensive to me and your father agrees."

"Will the boys live here, mamma?" Morgan asked.

"If they are not old enough to be fostered, then yes. Nevertheless, the boys have been given property of their own to manage upon your father's death. Rhiannon, you will have Hearthill Manor under the same stipulations that Morgan has with Seabridge."

"I love Hearthill Manor, mamma," Rhiannon said, looking shyly down at her lap. "I shall be happy there."

"I know, my love." Lady Pembridge smiled at her daughter who was only minutes younger than Morgan.

Morgan had recalled that her mother worried more about Rhiannon than the boys. And at one point her mother had asked her to always keep watch over her sister. Rhiannon had a tender heart and she was fragile in body and spirit.

"Morgan, this paragraph states that you will oversee Rhiannon's marriage contract giving her the same freedom as we have given to you to refuse a suitor. Rhiannon, Morgan will have the final say. I want you to have a good marriage, my love. Not one that will harm you. Sometimes love is blind leaving us vulnerable to those who would prey on us as women. This contract ensures that you will not be forced into a marriage that you do not want. It does not give you the freedom to marry who you want, unless it is an acceptable match. Do you understand the difference?"

"Yes, ma'am," Rhiannon acknowledged. "I am content to let Morgan chose," she said as her gaze drifted back out the window.

"Good. Morgan, if you are old enough to marry and James and John are still babies, then they will be under the care of your husband until they are ready to be fostered, so choose well."

"I shall choose a man just like Da," Morgan said with the confident lift of her chin.

"I could wish that for both of you, my loves. But men like your father who respect their wives and let them have a voice are rare. Not that they aren't out there. They are just hard to find."

"And if I do not marry?" Morgan asked, feeling that it was preferable never to marry than to marry and have the man she called husband not live up to the standard she had in her mind. James Morgan Pembridge was a shining example of a husband and father. She would settle for nothing less than a man who was his equal. Her Da was not perfect, but he was a God fearing man and he loved his family.

"I hope that you do find that man, Morgan. The love that I have found with your father and the joy my children give me is very fulfilling. But should you make the choice to remain unwed, then choose your steward wisely. Do not follow any man's counsel blindly, but take the counsel of several. Above all, Morgan, think for yourself." Lady Penbridge said, with a great deal of conviction.

"I don't know why we are even discussing this subject," Morgan remembered the feeling of dread that shot through her and she rose to her feet. "You and Da will be here to help me make a good match with a loving man who will adore me like Da adores you, and I shall give you a dozen grandchildren," Morgan said, feeling the blush rise in her cheeks.

"You are probably right but I want you to understand that life is not always fair, love, and fate can be cruel at times. Just remember that this contract exists."

Morgan acknowledged the terms of the agreement struck were not totally unprecedented. It is just not something done if other means were possible for management of an estate, and that usually entailed a marriage. At twenty, she understood the finer points of how society functioned. She understood what was and was not a cultural norm.

This was not the norm.

Furthermore, her father knew that it was unorthodox when he drafted the document at the insistence of her mother. Her father gave her mother everything her heart desired, so her mother hadn't needed to push very hard to get him to negotiate this agreement. Henry signed the agreement in September 1485, the first year of his rule and ascension to the throne.

Morgan was certain her uncle couldn't possibly know of the agreement's existence. Otherwise, the man would have had no qualms of forcing her into marriage years ago with a lackey of his own choosing before the king could object. It was certainly not to her uncle's advantage for her to reach her birthday unmarried.

However, in the meantime, Lester's greedy nature was playing into her plans. Knowing Lester was in no hurry to see her placed into the care of any husband, Morgan felt certain her uncle wouldn't release the reins of Seabridge quietly. She also had an epiphany three weeks back. Coming to terms with the fact that he would eventually reach the realization that she couldn't live if he was to keep Seabridge for himself, she knew that without hesitation the bastard would kill her. There was no one to stop him.

It was the catalyst she needed to bolster the courage to make her escape.

Her uncle wasn't going to control her any longer.

"I will go to King Henry and beg his indulgence for an audience," she said, firming up the plan in her mind to give her courage. Morgan wasn't quite sure how to go about that request, but she would figure it out. If he declined her audience or did grant the audience but declined her request outright, she would use the document. However, she was also smart enough to know it was never wise to push a king into a corner. She would allow Henry to select her husband and pray for the best.

And, in this instance, it was better to dance with the devil she didn't know than for her to continue this dance with the one she did.

She pushed down the fear. She pushed aside the uncertainty.

Tonight she was leaving it all behind, carrying nothing except her courage, a small sack of belongings, and the contract her mother had told her never to forget. That contract was between her father and the king.

It was a commitment that would truly set her free.

Chapter 3

In the distance Lord Lester Brentwood saw Seabridge sitting on the jagged cliffs. It was his Seabridge, or it would be soon enough and had been for the last seven years for all intents and purposes.

He had been gone for several months to escape the boredom of the long winter months and to sample the excitements London offered. Such diversions were not available on an isolated estate that sat on a piece of rock. He never would understand what his brother had seen in this hulking granite and limestone structure. Other than the wealth, he saw no advantages. However, he took the bad with the good. On the way back from London to Seabridge, he had decided to appoint an overseer and spend his days in London. Problem solved.

Bordering on the west coast of England, Seabridge was a fearsome enough place in summer; in winter, it was dreadful. With no company or entertainment, his boredom was complete. So he spent the Christmas season at the court of his king, Henry VII, and had decided to stay on past Easter, which was a bit longer than was his custom.

It was also a bit longer than he was welcome if Henry's response to his actions was to be believed.

Nevertheless, he was glad he had lingered, even if he wore out his welcome with Henry. Had he left when originally planned, he wouldn't have received the news until it was too late to counter the move the king was about to make in regard to his niece.

Henry had decided it was time for Morgan to marry and had promised her to a trusted knight on the king's short list of favorites. He knew the McKinnon man by reputation. The man wasn't one he would tangle with in a fair fight.

The man was of Viking descent, and that was obvious in both his build and his disposition.

Damn, he thought again.

He should have been expecting this after Henry forcefully declined his petition to marry her the previous summer. In retrospect, it had been a poor strategic move on his part. Henry denied him the right to his dead brother's daughter, and therefore, all her holdings. Making matters worse, he only succeeded in calling to the king's attention that Morgan was of marriageable age, wealthy, and still not betrothed.

Lester reasoned he would marry the girl himself and deal with the fallout and Henry's wrath. He'd claim ignorance and marry Morgan before Henry had a chance to publicize the formal arrangements. Then he'd be wealthy beyond his wildest dreams, which left him to wonder why he had not married her before now.

Besides, what could the king do after he compromised the girl? Henry was already angry with him, and no titled lord would have her once she was a used commodity. Such a man would be the laughing stock of the kingdom. The wealth and title of duke might be enough to soothe male egos, but he doubted it would be enough where the truly upper crust was concerned.

Lester smiled. His plans always worked one way or the other. Throw enough money, men, or threats at something, and it usually happened as planned.

Riding his prized Arabian into the courtyard and looking about, Lester wanted to be sure his groom was waiting to take his horse on his arrival at the stables.

"Gordon, I rode ahead," Lester said, looking down his nose at the servant. *For Christ's sake*, Lester thought, looking at Gordon. Lester wondered why the man was in rags and his face gaunt with hunger. Gordon had once been his dead brother's stable master, but Lester only allowed him to muck out the stalls. It was never a good thing to let a man have pride.

"Why are you not dressed properly?" Lester was haughty enough to ask such a question, never seeing his own responsibility in the decline of the once magnificent holding.

The stableman knew better than to reply that Lord Brentwood was an evil man and didn't take care of those under his watchful eye.

"Laundry day, sir," Gordon replied.

"See to it you don't look like this in public. You offend me," he said, bringing his handkerchief to his nose.

"Aye, sir." What else was he going to say?

"The supply wagon will be along shortly. Take care of my horse and, for God's sake, make sure you do it properly. I had to beat that stupid boy of yours the last time for failing to do as I directed. My horses are extremely valuable." Lester had spent a fortune of Morgan's money on his stables, reasoning that she would never miss it. "I trust you shall not make the same mistake?" Lester's voice, although soft, carried total authority.

"Nay, my lord, I'll not make the same mistake," Gordon spoke, his head bowed, his pride crushed years ago. Raising the anger of his overlord in any way was never a good idea. Any man brainless enough to cross this devil simply disappeared after being sent on an errand.

Lester hurried to the stronghold. Before the sun set, Seabridge would be his to do as he saw fit. His lifestyle would be no different from the past seven years, he mused. It would just be permanent. No one would dare to challenge his right to the holdings once he had married and properly bedded the Seventh Duchess.

"Bring Morgan and the priest to me at once!" he bellowed as he burst through the castle doors.

"Welcome home, Lord Brentwood," his housekeeper blurted, startled at his sudden return.

19

Lester smiled, sadistically feeding off Darcy's fear. She was afraid of him. Everyone was afraid of him. He knew the hold he had over the individuals in his charge. It gave him a thrill to know he had such power over their pathetic lives. He didn't care about them except that they serve. The outcome and consequences of poor action was his to dole out, and he did so in good measure.

"I wish ye had sent a messenger ahead. I could've seen to your meal," she prattled on nervously.

"Cease your babbling, Darcy, and go find the priest! Bring him and the girl to me in my solar at once."

At that same moment, Cyril stepped in from the courtyard. As Seabridge's captain of the guard, it was his duty to be the bearer of the news everyone had been dreading to deliver. It wasn't unheard of for bad news to result in the death of the one who delivered it.

"That directive is impossible to follow, sir."

Lester slowly turned to see who would dare to counter his demands. "And I await your answer as to why." His voice was cold as steel and dripped with sarcasm.

This is not good, Cyril thought. Not that he expected it to be. After all, this was Lord Brentwood he was facing.

"She's gone, sir," Cyril said flatly.

Lester's veins rose thick on his forehead and neck, giving Cyril the impression the devil was about to explode. Cyril had seen him angry many times before, and he feared for Darcy, who was standing too close to Lester for Cyril's comfort. Lord Brentwood was an evil man, never bothering to hide that personality trait. This far out in the borderlands between England and Wales, there was no one to stop him.

"Gone! What in the devil do you mean she's gone?"

His gaze hardened as he combed the foyer, waiting for an answer. No one was crazy or stupid enough to speak. The silence was deafening, but, more to the point, the silence was deadly.

Cyril spoke, breaking the silence that would bring more bad than good the longer the question went unanswered.

"Sir, we set the guard to watch the door. That said, we don't know how she escaped. She simply vanished. The best we can determine is it hasn't been more than three days based on the last time she ate."

"Have you been starving her? If I find that to be the case, I'll kill you myself for overstepping your boundaries." In his mind, he was the only one with the authority to punish her.

Darcy spoke, coming to Cyril's defense, "Oh no, sir, it wasn't our doing. It was Her Grace's choice. I swear on me mum's grave."

Darcy explained how Morgan refused to eat and had starved herself for some time. It didn't seem out of the ordinary that the duchess didn't touch her food for several days.

Cyril drew Lord Brentwood's gaze from his wife.

"On the third day, we went to give Her Grace some exercise as you had ordered, and the room was empty."

"What did she take with her?" Lester had to know what resources she had managed to steal from him.

"The only possession we know that disappeared around the same time was Demon."

"Demon?"

That was a surprise. Lester doubted Morgan could handle the magnificent beast, but if she were desperate enough, he supposed anything was possible.

"She could not have taken such a beast and managed him. I think it's just coincidence." Darcy made the mistake of offering her unsolicited opinion.

"I pay you to clean. I don't pay you to think!"

By this point, Lester was blood red in the face. Without warning, he backhanded Darcy and sliced her face open with his signet ring. The blow sent her to the polished stone floor. On reflex, the captain stepped forward to defend his wife. Lester drew his sword and ran the man through on the spot without warning or just cause in a sane man's mind.

Looking down, Lester watched in sadistic satisfaction as the blood began draining out of his guard. That crimson fluid slid like a serpent across the floor, pooling at his booted feet as if to point the way to the one who bore the guilt. While Darcy sobbed over Cyril's body, he kicked her like an errant dog nipping at his feet.

"You'll stop your infernal wailing at once and get this mess cleaned up, or I'll have you join your husband."

"Ye devil! I'll kill ye!" Darcy scrambled to her feet.

Lester was ready. Driving his dagger through her heart, he shoved it in to the hilt, then pushed her back to fall over her dead husband.

"Anyone else want to cross me?" Lester asked the staff that had gathered and looked on in horror. They began to scatter, not wanting to be the one he turned on next.

Lester grabbed a man by the arm before he could escape. "Toss their bodies over the cliff. They don't deserve a Christian burial. And you," he pointed to another, "have Stewart meet me in my solar!"

Taking the stairs two at a time, he headed up to the tower to see the room for himself. From the center of the cold and bleak cell, he made one slow turn.

The loss of his captain of the guard was an expensive turn of events, one he blamed entirely on Morgan. Her confinement was Cyril's responsibility.

Cyril had failed.

Morgan would pay once he got his hands around her slender throat. He smiled bitterly as he headed back downstairs to his solar. Yes, she would pay for a great many things, and, oh yes, she would pay in a great many ways.

Stewart Whittaker stood facing the fireplace as Brentwood entered. With his hands behind his back, he studied the oversized portrait of the Fifth Duke of Seabridge, Lord Brentwood's stepfather.

Stewart resented the feeling the painting gave him. It was as if even from the grave, the Fifth Duke was lording over him, mocking everything he had ever tried to become, knowing all the while he had fallen short in the eyes of this great man.

Slowly, Stewart turned.

"I understand you need my services," he said softly. Choosing to never draw attention to himself, Stewart found it to his benefit to hold an appearance of servitude.

Lester took a brief survey of the man, noting Stewart's modest dress and clean-cut appearance. Lester had always sensed something familiar about the man; even the very first day they had met, he thought he should know him from somewhere. He couldn't put his finger on it, and he usually didn't dwell on it, feeling more important things needed his attention and efforts than why Stewart struck a familiar cord.

In his opinion, Stewart wasn't a man most would think to fear on first glance. He was sure such an advantage was useful for him and was the primary secret to his success in his chosen profession. However, appearances could be most deceiving. He was a man that Lester was glad to have in his pocket and not another's. Moreover, there was always a place for such an asset as Stewart. He was ruthless, uncaring, and almost without a soul in Lester's mind. Lester easily found a place for him at Elderage Castle and then Seabridge, keeping Lester's hands clean as Stewart did the dirty work.

Lester largely doubted Stewart was his real name. Besides, who was asking? He surely wasn't. When Stewart had appeared eight years ago with no explanation of who he was or why he chose to grace Elderage Castle with his presence, Lester briefly wondered who he might be. However, Lester stopped caring almost immediately on Stewart's arrival. The man possessed a bag full of neat little tricks, which were extremely useful at times just like this. He had discovered the man to be most worthwhile. So, his true identity failed to matter.

Lester nodded. "Aye, I find myself in need of your special skill set. It seems my disobedient and most ungrateful niece has seen fit to flee the confines of my tender care."

Stewart snorted. "Tender care, indeed," he mumbled under his breath. "Imagine that."

Lester ignored the comment as he pulled a locked metal box from his desk drawer. "I need you to find her and bring her back before the king gets wind that she has fled."

Or more importantly in Lester's mind, he needed to get her back before her would-be husband arrived at his doorstep, demanding his rights by royal decree. An ugly encounter that would prove to be, he felt certain. He was capable of defending himself under usual circumstances, but Henry's knight wasn't usual. A huge man with a natural ability to dominate on the battlefield, Nic McKinnon would make him his plaything.

"I must have her back, wed and bedded before the knight arrives. I don't care to have an encounter with the man."

Lester could see from the look on Stewart's face that he actually found the thought amusing and might be willing to stick around to watch the predictable outcome. Nevertheless, Lester had other plans for Stewart's time.

"You have my permission to use any and every means available to you, Stewart. My only stipulation is you're not to openly beat her if she's uncooperative. And you know she will be." He was beginning to think he might go with

Stewart after all. The prospect of hunting her down and tying her up had a nice feel to it.

Stewart shrugged. "Ensuring her cooperation won't be a problem."

Lester was quite certain that Stewart had his ways of ensuring obedience.

"Good," Lester said.

Leaning over the large desk once belonging to his brother, he handed his puppet a leather pouch heavy with the coins that he had pulled from the strongbox.

"Her condition upon return?" Stewart asked, lacking any real emotion that might betray his true feelings on the subject.

"I only need her alive. Other than that," Lester gestured with a dismissive wave of his hand, "I don't care what condition I find her in on her return." He watched as Stewart continued to stare at him. "Were my orders clear?"

"Aye, they're clear."

"Then why are you still standing here?" Lester got the feeling when he looked at Stewart that something wasn't quite right with the man. *Perhaps this needs to be his last job*, Lester thought. When Stewart returned, it might be wise to allow him to inspect the castle bowels and become a permanent resident there through some unfortunate accident. "Was there something else?" Lester added as Stewart continued to return his gaze.

"I need you to send out a large complement of men to search for her. Make sure they are visible," Stewart commanded a little more forcefully than intended.

"Why?" Lester asked, suspicious of Stewart's motives.

Lester caught the look. Stewart wasn't quick enough to cover his irritation in the questioning of his tactics.

"I want the larger party as a diversion to cover my own activities. I will track her myself. I find one man can go where many men cannot."

Lester nodded. "Consider it done. I'll dispatch them immediately," Lester said, satisfied with the reasoning to expend resources.

"Then with that, I take my leave."

Stewart turned to leave by the double door and walked soundlessly across the lush carpets, spoils from the Crusades fought by some long-forgotten ancestor.

"Stewart?" Lester questioned, then paused, lending greater weight to his final word. He waited for Stewart to turn around. He needed to reassert his dominance. "Do not return without her."

Stewart nodded in understanding before softly closing the door.

Shortly after Stewart's leaving, Lester scanned the room from behind the elegantly carved desk. He had come to think of all this as his own. He had been guardian and overseer of Seabridge for seven years. He had been lord and master since the fire that had killed his older brother. Now, he was going to have it all. It was going to be his if it was the last thing he did. It was just a matter of time.

Chapter 4

"What was I thinking!" Morgan screamed as the magnificent black stallion barreled uncontrollably towards the rubble of the old Roman wall. She was certainly seeing that the decision to take Demon had been extremely reckless regardless of her need for speed and agility in navigating any obstacles she expected to encounter.

The stallion gracefully leaped the wall with little wasted effort, unseating his slight burden in the process and throwing her clear of the stone barrier, straight into the bog flanking the path. Morgan felt the blow to her head as her body shook with the impact of her landing.

Feeling the shadows of oblivion dragging her into the abyss, Morgan ceased to care.

The sun was shining and she was free.

It was a good day to die.

~*****~

Nic caught a glimpse of the young rider out of the corner of his eye. Now focused on the movement, he saw through the trees a black stallion leap over the ruins of some Roman fortification deserted hundreds of years ago and forgotten by time and man. He also saw the rider go flying through the air, landing with a potentially deadly impact on ground strewn with rock and rubble, before the young man rolled a few feet and fell into a shallow bog. The boy was going under just as he arrived. Nic pulled him out and checked for a pulse.

"Good, he lives," Nic said after satisfying himself that there was a heartbeat.

"Ummmm."

Nic heard the boy groan softly in pain. He eased his touch. "Hold still, lad. Moving around will only increase the discomfort." Nic continued to hover over the lad. "Let me have a feel. Now, hold still just a minute more. By the way, I'm Sir Nic McKinnon," he offered as he continued his inspection, hoping the gift of his name would foster trust. "I'll not harm you, lad." Nic didn't know if the boy was coherent enough to hear him and understand. The lad had taken a nasty blow to the head and had yet to fully open his eyes.

The disembodied voice floated over Morgan as she remained still.

Strange how the arms of death are so comforting, she thought. It was almost as if she could feel them, tangible and inviting. *Did the Grim Reaper talk, too?* she wondered. If so, with a voice like his, no wonder some craved death, welcoming it with open arms. Again she wished for the dark nothingness.

It wasn't to be.

Slowly the effects of the fall were receding, giving way to realization that she wasn't dying and this wasn't the Grim Reaper. She was in the arms of a strange man whose name she thought was Nic. She knew his strong, capable hands running down her arms satisfied him that there were no broken bones.

Wisely, Morgan held still.

Resisting the urge to bat his hands away wasn't a battle easily won for her, and she wasn't sure that battle was over. No one ever touched her except to cause her pain, yet she could see his touch was utilitarian with no malice intended. Still, the impulse to flee was overpowering. Upon closer reflection, Morgan conceded that the fear of this giant man and what he might or might not do to her was a far distant second to her fear of discovery or him forcing her back to Seabridge.

If she spoke at this point, he would realize two things: she wasn't hurt and she was not a boy. The ruse might work at a distance, but close inspection might find her disguise lacking credence. If the knight discovered she was, in reality, the duchess of Seabridge, he would send her back. He would have no choice. The law was clear, and he would never believe that doing so would be to deliver her truly into the arms of death.

She glanced at him. Death by her uncle's hands would never look like this man regardless of her thoughts just moments earlier.

She wasn't going to delude herself. The beating she would receive for this escape would be severe. The punishments had been getting more violent and frequent over the last year. With this escape attempt, she had just given her uncle the excuse he needed to kill her should he ever get his hands on her again.

She could never go back. Not while Lester was alive.

Years as a soldier had finely honed Nic's senses. He noticed the pulse racing in the hollow of the boy's throat. He smelled the boy's fear and knew the young man would try to run at the first opportunity. Nic's conscience, slight as it might be in many instances, wouldn't allow him to leave the filthy, skinny creature until he was sure the lad was fit to travel alone. He would be easy pickings if someone was set on evil.

"Easy, easy, I'll not harm you," Nic repeated. His words were softly laced with the influences of his deceased Scottish mother. His home was just two miles south of the Scottish territorial border. Hence the surname of McKinnon. Apparently, somewhere back in time, loyalties were blurred. His were not. Yet, even if his loyalties were firmly set in Henry's court, it didn't change the fact he sounded like neither an Englishman or a Scot. It had caused him much angst through his career in Henry's service. The Scots felt he was a turncoat, and the English trusted him only as far as they could toss him, until they got to know him. Those who did know him never doubted his love for his king and country. At this point Nic would never dream of defying his king even given his Scottish roots.

"You're lucky nothing's broken, but rest assured, my young friend, you'll be verray sore. It was lucky for you that I happened along to pull you out of the mire before you went completely under."

Nic waited for acknowledgment. There was none forthcoming, making him suspect the boy was more injured than any outward appearance might suggest.

"Can you speak, lad?" Nic asked.

Morgan was fully awake and mesmerized by the soothing voice of her rescuer. His face was only inches from hers, and she thought it was the most handsome she had ever seen. He was in his late twenties. His jaw was square and his lips wide and sensual. Below that tempting mouth was a deep cleft in his chin, keeping his lips from seeming overly soft. She had the inexplicable urge to pull his face closer to test the softness for herself.

However, his eyes struck her the most. Those pools of brown reflected the real depths of the man thinly veiled by cynicism and worldly knowledge. *He may be young*, she thought, *but he has seen much*.

He was a seasoned warrior, undoubtedly hardened by endless battles and loss, which only added to his appeal.

She shook her head as if to clear her thoughts. It was a mistake. That action sent the world spinning.

Nic saw the color drain from the lad's face. He had seen it before. Head injury and vomiting went hand in hand.

"You're going to be sick," Nic said as a matter of fact. His reaction time was quick; his movements done with little care given. Turning the boy to his side, he kept the lad's breakfast off his boots.

"Don't swallow it. Rinse and spit," he said, handing the boy some water. "Better?"

Nic observed the lad shake his head in the negative, spit the water out and then vomit again. This time Nic wasn't quick enough to have it miss his boots.

"Och! Well, 'tis nay a first time," he said with a sigh as he shook it off.

Nic also realized the boy didn't apologize or speak. There could be several logical reasons for his silence besides simply being an ingrate. Not that he was ruling it out at this point. Could be the boy had a deep lack of trust or was in shock. More likely the boy just was incapable of speech.

"Are you mute, lad?"

Morgan jumped at the opening that the knight unknowingly provided her. It was a brilliant cover and one she wouldn't have considered. If he thought she couldn't speak, it would keep her from having to answer any questions. She had no idea how long the ruse might hold up, but even a day would buy her time.

Impulsively, she nodded. The slight movement cost her dearly as the world began to spin again.

"Ahhh," she let the sound of agony slip past her lips. She grabbed the collar of his light leather armor and hung on to make the world slow down.

"You need to move slowly. Give yourself a chance to recover," Nic said as he stood up and extended his hand.

Sitting on the soft, moist earth, Morgan looked at one of the largest men she had ever seen.

She studied his extended hand that was offered in assistance. She hesitated to take it, knowing all deeds come with a price and wondering what the price would be for accepting this knight's offer of help.

"Fate is knocking at the door, Morgan. Answer it," the voice of her mother seemed to speak to her. So, placing her trust in fate, she placed her hand in his.

Chapter 5

Dusting off his hands, Nic was ever alert to any danger lurking. It wasn't unheard of for highwaymen to set traps using just such tactics and attack while the unsuspecting Good Samaritan had his back turned, distracted by the decoy.

However, if the boy's a decoy, he's a good one, Nic thought.

"Will family be looking for you, lad?" Nic asked, helping the lad to his feet.

The boy shook his head, never meeting Nic's gaze.

Nic inclined his head to the stallion grazing just up the ridge. "Did you steal him?"

He doubted the boy would be honest, but it would give him opportunity to judge his reaction to the question. Body language always told Nic more than words alone.

Now, he looked him square in the eye.

Well now, Nic thought, *this boy is angry*. He found it slightly amusing considering the company the young man was in at the moment.

Nic held up his hands in a gesture of concession, amused at the fight he saw in his new charge. "Now, my young friend, just be at ease. It's a fair question. It's not often I come across someone where ownership doesn't hinge on possession being eleven points in the law, and they say there are but twelve," he said, then smiled as he remembered the ancient Scottish proverb.

Nic turned away from the boy, looking toward the stallion, with his hands planted on his hips, long muscular legs spread wide. That was one fine piece of horseflesh. Turning back, Nic looked at his new traveling companion and knew instinctively this urchin was in need, no matter how rich the horse.

Nic was also in need. Maybe fate was feeling generous today.

"I find my choice of traveling light and without a squire is proving to be a poor decision. If you wish, you can act as my squire until we get to my home in the north."

He assured the boy that after they arrived, if he wanted to stay, he could find something for him to do. There was always plenty of work for an honest set of hands. He agreed to pay a modest allowance and offered protection. In return, his expectation was to take care of his horse, attend his needs, and obey his directions always and without question.

"Do we have an agreement?" Nic asked, all banter aside. An agreement was an agreement, and he would hold up his end as long as the young man held to his.

The boy nodded.

"Excellent, we agree then." Nic gathered his horse and brought the stallion back with surprising ease. "However, first, I have a stop to make. I have to tie up some business, and then we're on to my lands just south of the border of Scotland. Unfortunately, this business can't wait," Nic said, then pursed his lips. "Nasty business, too," he said under his breath, caring not if the lad heard him.

King Henry wanted him to marry. That was the nasty business, but necessary when the king decrees it, Nic supposed. He had no real desire to take a wife and never had wanted a wife as far back as he could remember. However, one doesn't disobey a king and live comfortably to tell of it. Consequently, he would marry.

Living with his bride had not been one of Henry's stipulations.

He knew it was a technicality, and one that Henry would eventually see through. However, until that time came, he was still a free man.

"I need to stop at Seabridge," Nic said as he turned to mount his horse.

Morgan felt her jaw drop. She had agreed to act as the knight's squire because he said they were heading north. It was in the opposite direction from London. Nevertheless, Morgan had faith. She would get to London eventually, and her uncle would never think to look for her in the northern country. It would give her time to regroup. And survive past her twenty-first birthday.

But now Sir Nic was going to Seabridge?

Oh, no, she thought. Not after all she went through to escape. She would kill herself before letting her uncle get his hands on her again. The end result would be the same; she would just make it quicker.

Nic saw the color drain away and panic play across the boy's face.

Seabridge's stables were legendary. The horse was magnificent. It came together for him in a single thought: *that horse belongs to Lord Brentwood.*

Yet there could be another logical explanation besides theft. However, if the boy's a thief, there would be hell to pay, he thought. Stealing from Lester Brentwood would be a death sentence for a boy like this one. Moreover, Nic bet such a death would be slow and agonizing. The pleasure would only be one-sided.

"You're afraid." Nic knew it was an understatement. Terror poured off this boy in waves.

The boy nodded, dropping his gaze to the forest floor, he squeezed his eyes tightly against the very fear Nic so accurately and acutely saw in him.

"Why? Surely, monsters don't live there, but only mere flesh and bone which can be conquered. I've met Lord Brentwood, and even though his dealings are a bit severe for my taste, he has a reputation of being fair when dealing with his tenants." Nic wasn't so sure that reputation was still accurate.

The boy shook his head slowly. Nic no longer wondered if there was a monster that lurked under the surface of fine silk and velvet.

Nic took the boy by the shoulders. "If there is no just cause, son, I'll see to it he never touches you. But, I need to know and I need you to be honest. Did you steal that horse?"

The boy shook his head again before placing his hand over his heart in a gesture Nic understood to be a promise of the truthfulness of his words and softly patted his chest as to say he's mine.

"All right, for some strange reason, I believe you." Nic looked him square in the eyes. Then he cocked his head to the side in thought. "Will I be forced to surrender you or defend you, lad?"

Morgan knew it was a rhetorical question. They both knew surrender or defense was inevitable.

Nic dropped his hands from the boy's shoulders with a sigh. "The day's not getting any younger. Whether I like it or not, I must go. Can you show me the quickest route and trust that I'll keep you safely out of the way?"

Morgan nodded.

Fate had stepped in for her and she seized the opportunity. If he didn't know the way, she would lead him as far from his destination as possible. Every step to the east was another step closer to true freedom. She had no idea what she would face on the journey ahead.

More precisely, she didn't care.

The unknown was exactly that, the unknown. She knew for certain what she was leaving behind.

For her it would be certain death.

Chapter 6

The sun was low in the sky when Nic finally stopped to rest their horses. They had been steadily making their way inland. They were far enough inland that the trees were thickening, the underbrush growing to a dense mass of tangles. They had long since left the coastal region, moving on a steady path eastward.

He knew it.

He just didn't care where they were heading because neither one of them wanted to go to Seabridge for two very different reasons. So, yes, he knew. And if the sun that was setting to his back hadn't tipped him off, then the fact he could no longer smell the sea did. However, he continued to let this young lad lead the way. He was in no real hurry to meet his new bride. She had been in Brentwood's care for seven years, what were a couple more days?

He was also curious about this youngster. He was almost too pretty to be a boy, and he had such long and graceful limbs. Nic had never had a passion for young boys; nevertheless, the boy inexplicably drew him. Something just didn't feel right, and time would tell, he felt certain. Time had taught Nic to listen to his gut when it spoke, and that gut was telling him there was something he was missing.

Up ahead and unaware of his scrutiny, Morgan was having issues of her own. Her headache was proving a distraction from the man who blindly followed her lead. She had almost forgotten he was even there.

"I introduced myself earlier, but I'm not sure you remember. I'm Sir Nic McKinnon. Do you have a name, lad?" Nic asked, bringing his warhorse alongside to her own yet keeping a respectable distance between the two beasts.

The message Morgan tried to convey was a cross between, "That is a dumb question" and "For God's sake, don't distract me while I'm trying to keep from falling on my bum."

Nic almost laughed. "Of course you have a name. Are you able to write your letters? If not, then I'll just give you a name you like. However, if you can write, then spell your name out on my hand." They stopped in the road, and Nic held out his palm.

Nodding, Morgan reached across and took his hand in hers. Taking a deep breath, she rolled the dice. Banking on him never putting the Duchess of Seabridge and the dirty, scruffy peasant together as one in the same, she wrote and then looked at him.

"M... O... R... G... A... N... Morgan," Nic said, rolling the name round on his tongue. "A good Welsh name. I believe it means Sea-Born."

Then realization came as he sat on his warhorse, striking him like a physical blow. Nic hoped the revelation wasn't reflected in his face. Could this waif staring at him be his sea-born bride? Was this dirty, scruffy urchin the prize for his long and faithful service to the king? What had he done recently to anger Henry to the point that his king would pawn this woman off on him? The list of possible actions was actually pretty long when he really gave it thought. Still, he had never known Henry to be petty or vindictive in his punishment when he had pissed him off. Nic supposed there was always a first.

Then he stilled his mind. He let the emotion of the moment go and looked at her, staring into the beautiful green eyes, too large for her overly thin face. He looked past the shortly cropped hair that was as dark as the deepest midnight. Looking past the dirt, he took in the high cheekbones, the perfect bone structure of her delicate features.

He had no doubt she was a female. The soft curves barely discernible under the groom's clothing just clinched the argument he was having with himself.

All right, he thought, *I'll play along for now and see where this takes us.*

She obviously had some reason to run and take on a disguise to do it. Had King Henry's decree reached her and she fled out of fear of him? Nic was aware of his far-flung reputation. He knew he was the best in the king's forces.

Men sought him out to fight, always thinking to topple him from his standing. Women at court sought after him for vastly different reasons. The air of danger and emotional unavailability hanging about him was a mighty lure, proving irresistible to many.

However, those attachments came with a price that Nic was never willing to pay.

He figured if he wanted a close, meaningful relationship, he would get another horse.

No, he thought. *The notion of going back to Seabridge singularly terrified her.* He could see it in her eyes. She wasn't running from him, but from a more terrifying predator. Lord Brentwood or someone at the castle was the only explanation that he could reason out. Why else would a young woman of her standing be willing to risk life on the run as opposed to a safe and comfortably pampered lifestyle behind castle walls?

He had heard rumors the last few months of Brentwood's unusual tastes in the bedroom and tales of unfortunate women who had to have physicians summoned after a night spent in Lord Brentwood's company. Nic knew the nobleman's tastes had become more perverted and physically violent. So much so that Henry asked him to leave the court shortly after he himself left.

Nevertheless, surely Lester wouldn't be so idiotic as to misuse his ward. Such a notion was inconceivable even to a hardened soldier like him. Common court whores were one thing, and even that he didn't approve. Morgan was certainly not in that category of woman. She was a gentle woman born and bred. She was a duchess, for Christ's sake, and short of a princess, it didn't get much higher a birth.

What was more to the point was that kind of abuse would bring on King Henry's rage. Henry was widely known for his kindness to women and tolerated little of that kind of behavior in or of his subjects. Lester Brentwood was already teetering on the wrong side of Henry's good graces, and the king had personally placed Morgan in the care of her uncle with the express promise that her well-being be seen to at all costs. If Nic found the situation to be otherwise, the hell and fire that would rain down on Brentwood would soon become legendary. Nic didn't have his reputation for no good reason.

However, before Nic could continue his train of thought, his battle-honed senses piqued. Sensing the danger, Nic reacted even before feeling the hoofbeats tearing up ground at breakneck speed. A complement of no fewer than ten men, by his estimation, were nearly on them. Jumping from his horse, he dragged her along with him.

"Don't make a sound," he commanded as he hurried his young charge and their mounts into the woods as deeply as possible to avoid detection.

Morgan was too frightened to react. Frozen in fear, he pulled her back against him. Placing one arm around her waist with the horse's reins still held tightly in his fist, she felt him place his other hand over her mouth. Quickly realizing his mistake, Nic pulled his hand away but didn't release her. She couldn't have made a sound if she wanted to, but she just might run. Nic couldn't chance it. It was classic fight or flight, and flight was his bet at the moment.

"Ease your breathing, Morgan. They're on us," Nic whispered in her ear. She felt the heated breath as the soft-spoken words touched her, and their meaning was clear.

Nic went deadly still, freezing in place.

So did Morgan.

Morgan held her breath as two columns of horses passed no more than twenty feet from their hiding place, pushing their mounts at a speed that would eventually kill the animals.

Damn them! she thought. *They're going to kill my horses!* Morgan took a step toward them.

Nic jerked her back. "Let them go."

So the search has begun, he thought.

Her thoughts mirrored his. The search was on.

It was obvious to Morgan they knew she was gone. The fantasy of her escaping without someone noticing was exactly that, a fantasy. Obviously, her uncle was back at the castle.

Morgan realized that if she couldn't control her fear, it would control her. So she told herself she wouldn't feel fear, not any more. Anger made her less of a victim, and she refused to be that any longer. She let her anger roil within her. She let the dark emotion spring up in her so sharply that she began to tremble uncontrollably with the force and desire to kill her uncle. She hated Lester for having no regard for any life, animal or human.

Nic, still clutching her to him, felt this reaction to the search party, saw her gray and drawn features, and cursed under his breath. He counted twelve men in total, each bearing the blue and gold flying dragon. It was the crest of the Duchess of Seabridge.

A fierce and foreign feeling settled within him.

He was a knight of the realm, by God, sworn to protect the king and his subjects.

However, above all else, he would allow no one to harm what belonged to a McKinnon, and she was his for better or worse.

"We can't remain on the main road if there's a search party already on the loose. Come," he said, taking her by the hand. "We'll double back the way we came and follow the stream rather than the roadway," Nic stated with a bit more anger than warranted. If he had doubts about the origins of her concerns, those were put to rest. No one sends out that large of a search party for a petty horse thief.

They needed to find a safe haven to make camp and soon. Darkness was descending rapidly, and he had no desire to be out in the open after dark. The search party was only a small part of the necessity to find shelter.

Blindly, Morgan followed, not questioning his decision to place her in front of him on his mount. Fearing Demon was being left behind in the haste to put distance between them and the search party, Morgan glanced back to be sure he was behind them. Losing him would leave her completely at Nic's mercy. She saw that Nic was aware of her movements, and Morgan guessed correctly that he understood her concern. The animal was her freedom.

"He's still with us, lad," Nic reassured her.

Quickening the pace, Nic turned them around, doubling back on their previous path. It would cost them valuable time; nevertheless, the action was necessary if he was going to successfully skirt the men set on taking Morgan back to a place she obviously didn't want to be.

Veering off the road and moving into the woods, Nic followed the stream that he had heard earlier running parallel to the road. It seemed the most prudent action since pushing forward wasn't an option.

It was nearing dark when he found an ideal grove of trees to make camp for the night.

Fate is still feeling generous, he thought.

Nic was aware that Morgan had quickly decided it was in her best interest to follow his lead without question, and he counted his blessings. He needed to be free of distraction if he were to keep them alive. At this point, he didn't look or smell any better than she did and could quite easily be misconstrued as her kidnapper.

42

Again, Nic doubted his decision to travel alone and without backup. His friend Connor had almost insisted on joining him, but he had refused. And now Connor wasn't with him, and Nic would have to make do. He prayed his cockiness didn't cost Morgan her life.

He dismounted, pulling Morgan down after him. He spoke quietly, knowing voices carry on the wind.

"See to the horses. I'll make camp."

Morgan nodded. She had some idea of what to do. The rest she would muddle through. She figured acting like she knew what she was doing was half the battle won.

Nic didn't waste energy or time gathering firewood. There wouldn't be a fire tonight, he decided. Firelight and the smell of smoke might draw attention they didn't need.

"I have cold meat, cheese, and bread in the right side of the saddle pack. Bring it once you water and feed the mounts."

Morgan looked around and tentatively touched his sleeve to gain his attention. She looked up into his eyes, smiled, and nodded in approval of the spot he had chosen for them to pass the night. Nic felt his toes curl at the transformation of her face.

Good Lord, he thought. Nic feared that if she flashed that dimpled smile at the wrong time, they would be in big trouble. There wasn't a soul who wouldn't see through her disguise.

"Morgan, go tend our horses. The hour grows late." Not waiting for her answer, Nic turned her in the direction of the stream.

Standing at the edge of the stream, Morgan wholeheartedly agreed with his choice. To her untrained eye, the area was beautiful. How was she to know that for Nic it was simply the most defensible fortification he could find on short notice?

After flailing around in the bog, she needed a bath but settled for washing what muck she could off her arms and face without getting in the water. Full immersion would have to wait; the horses came first.

As directed, she began to gather the tall grass from around the stream, surveying her surroundings as she went. Just because she couldn't bathe, didn't mean she couldn't appreciate the beauty around her. It was a lovely spot. The clear water was gently running, bubbling and soothing as the last of the birds began seeking their roosts for the night. The trees seemed enchanted and gave her a sense of wonder, as she had never seen trees so large with their canopies reaching heavenward, and trunks so wide it would take four grown men with arms stretched wide to surround them. It was an ancient, enchanted place and she wanted to stay here forever.

Turning in circles, Morgan tossed her head back and spread her arms wide as if trying to touch the treetops. Laughing for the first time in ages, she fell dizzy to the ground.

Nic watched her from a safe distance, marveling at the joy so obvious on her face at just being here in this beautiful place.

When had he lost that capacity?

When had he last possessed the ability to be in awe of the beauty of nature? When had he lost the joy to live for the moment, not worry about the past, or fret about what he couldn't change, or keep reaching for a future that wasn't yet set? When had he stopped accepting, or worse, stopped noticing the small joys life had to offer.

He couldn't recall.

His life had not been his own since joining the service of his king. Life had evolved into nothing more than one battle after another of either wits or strength. There had been precious little time for smelling the flowers, figuratively or literally. Was he jealous of the childlike innocence he sensed in his bride? No, not precisely.

44

"Pffff," he huffed at himself. He didn't have time for this. *Let her dream for both of us,* he thought as he went about securing the camp. He had to keep them alive.

Chapter 7

Morgan tethered the beautiful stallions to a low branch and brought back the meal for Nic. Her senses were on high alert as she took the bread, salted meat, and cheese to him. She found him sitting in a relaxed position.

Looks can be deceiving, she thought.

Morgan noticed what many might not. Time had honed her senses, too, from vastly different means than Nic's, but to the same end result: to keep her alive.

His back was up against an oak so gnarled and ancient it must have seen King Arthur's reign, with one long leg stretched out in front of him and the other drawn up, bent at the knee. His forearm rested comfortably on that knee, his sword was within easy reach. It would have surprised her more if his weapon had not been close at hand.

Cautiously, she made her way over to his side and extended the offering. Getting no closer than necessary made her feel better. Somewhere on the surface of her mind, she understood it would take more than an arm's length to keep her safe should he decide he wanted to hurt her.

Nic looked up at her, noticing her wary posture, and wondered why she was so skittish. It went beyond shy.

"Thank you," he said. As he reached for the food he covered her hand with his.

That contact was brief, but she involuntarily jerked back, dropping the small plate before he had a secure grip.

A deep sound arose in Nic's throat, hot and intense at whoever had abused this delicate creature so much that she pulled away from human touch. Morgan moved back even farther, eyes wide with extreme caution at her misstep. She wasn't necessarily afraid of him, she realized. He didn't scare her to the point of being frozen in fear. That was good, she supposed. Actually, Morgan wasn't really sure how she felt with him; she was just ready for anything.

Nic gritted his teeth. "My anger isn't toward you, Morgan, but at the circumstances that would leave you so mistrusting."

He saw her hesitation but also the relief and maybe confirmation of what he hoped she already knew. Then again, maybe it was his hope.

"I promised to take care of you, and I'll do so. Now, eat." Nic pointed to the food. Lucky for him it was on his blanket and not on the bare ground. The nourishment was too precious to waste. He had only packed provisions for one. And, even if in the past he had eaten some very questionable things out of necessity, it wasn't his preference.

She shook her head. Never taking her eyes off him, she took another step back. Morgan stared at her new lord, not daring to blink. He didn't frighten her as much as he distressed her. Simply put, he was intimidating. It was obvious to her what she saw in him was the potential for a dangerous man.

Intuitively, Morgan knew the danger in him went well beyond anything she had ever seen in her uncle. This was a man accustomed to command. He wore that aura visibly. Nic McKinnon was a man who was shrewd. He was, in a word, deadly to an enemy. Yet, somehow, she also knew that he would protect anything he felt worthy of his efforts. Did he now consider her worthy?

"Aye, Morgan, you will eat," he commanded softly. "You promised to follow my instructions back at the old Roman wall. Did you not?"

Nic waited for her to acknowledge his question.

She nodded. She did agree at the time and felt certain it was still a smart move. After all, he did manage to get them safely away from the search party.

"I'm your overlord now, and you will submit to my judgment in any action which is to your greater good." Nic waited for Morgan to take the food.

But she was rooted to the spot. Nic stood.

Oh my, she thought, understanding that she had crossed some imaginary line with him.

"Eat, Morgan." His voice had dropped to a rough whisper.

He had succeeded in shaking her to depths far greater than her uncle, with his rafter-raising tirades, had ever done. He took a step forward. Morgan stood her ground, straightened her back, and held her head high before taking the food he offered. And after her meager display of bravado, she also made for a little safer distance from him.

As she ate, she took the opportunity to pilfer a look at Nic and found him distant and deep in thought. She wondered what a man like him gave his mental energies to?

Women? Maybe, but not in this instance.

Gambling? Probably not.

Hanging his enemies from the tallest tree? Now, that she would believe.

Morgan's mind was racing. She didn't know this man. What if he sought out the search party and turned her over to them? She was certain her uncle would pay dearly to have her returned. But she shook the thought away. He could have done that already.

What sort of man was he? she wondered.

Could her uncle bribe him? No, she felt not.

Still, he was worth watching. Every man was worth watching. Nic was no exception.

She took this opportunity to take a closer look at him physically. He was tall by modern standards and broad through the shoulders. Her father had been a tall man. However, her father's coloring had been light blond to Nic's dark good looks. Her mother had told her once that her father was a descendant of the Vikings. Those marauders of the island eventually settled, assimilating into the local culture. She would be very surprised if Nic didn't have some Viking ancestry in his lineage. Men of his stature certainly didn't come along every day.

Nic's size didn't intimidate her in the least. His height made her feel protected and safe, much as when her father was alive. It was a feeling that Morgan had long ago forgotten and realized she missed. Nonetheless, she would experience this feeling from a distance, but not up close.

From an artist's perspective his proportions were perfect and beautifully pulled together. Nature got it right where this one was concerned, and she would love to do a charcoal rendering of him on his equally magnificent horse. Morgan doubted that she would get him to sit still long enough to accomplish much more than a rough sketch.

His arms and legs were long and well-muscled from the years of fighting and training. It stood to reason that his shoulders would be toned and chiseled. Upper body strength was necessary for any warrior. It was a given. Hauling sixty-five pounds of armor around on one's body and being able to move in it like it was a second skin would require body development out of sheer necessity.

There was no extra fat on him.

His hands were large and tan. He had long fingers with clean nails that were free of the grime most fighting men sported. She knew Nic could kill her with one blow if he decided to. However, he didn't strike her as a man who would use brute strength to subdue his opponent, unlike her uncle. He would use cunning, stealth, and strategy, which would brilliantly complement his strength. She wondered if that strength would come across in a drawing. It would prove challenging.

His leather boots and overclothes were well made and of good quality, even if quite dirty from his effort to pull her from the bog. He was obviously a man of means. If his clothes didn't hint at that understated wealth, then his sword and mount certainly said as much. The saddle and tack for that magnificent animal were worth twenty times what the average farm tenant earned in his lifetime.

Her protector's hair was clean but long overdue for a trim. Certainly his hairstyle—and she used that term *style* very loosely—was much longer than what currently was in fashion. Judging by her uncle's hair, the nobility at court were wearing theirs just below the ear.

Yet the longer locks suited Nic, reminding Morgan of a story her mother told her as a child. The character named Samson was of Herculean strength. The secret to his strength was in his long hair. She knew this wasn't the case with Nic. Yet it was still an amusing thought that took her back to a happier time when her mother would read to her and her twin sister in the hour before bedtime.

No, Nic's strength surely came courtesy of years of fighting, and he was more likely a man who tossed fashion to the wind, not giving a care of what high society thought of him.

Morgan knew that beneath the calm surface lay a powerful man and it had nothing to do with his hair.

It surprised her that she had the urge to go to him and smooth back the lock falling over his forehead. She guessed if she had to have a benefactor, it was best to have one who could back his claims of protection. Morgan instinctively knew not to doubt this man's ability to support such a claim. She found this revelation to be reassuring.

Little escaped Nic's attention; he was aware of her taking stock of him. He knew, even if there was a more relaxed smile on her face, there was no blind trust in her. If she came to trust him, it was because he had earned her trust.

It will come in time, he told himself.

Nic pulled himself up from his resting place after finishing his evening meal where he had spent a good deal of time mulling over his problem of having a skittish runaway bride with a large search party in hard pursuit. Nic knew the day had gone downhill quickly. The only plus was she was eating. That certainly couldn't hurt her, considering she was thin as a corn stalk.

"If you thought to bring a blanket, I suggest you go get it from your pack." Nic looked up at the cloudless evening sky. "It's going to be a cold night."

Morgan couldn't dispute that observation, having slept years in just such cold and dampness.

"We'll have no fire to keep warm or to keep the forest animals at bay," Nic said softly, coming to stand by her. "We should sleep close to share body warmth."

This is something new, she thought. Morgan had never slept under the stars. However, she had dreamed of how it could be. Many times, she dreamed of this very freedom as she stared beyond her tower window far into the night, its darkness broken only by distant, twinkling stars.

She jumped up and quickly brought back her cloak from her bag as well as the baby-fine woolen blanket she had judiciously packed, both items found in a trunk in the room that was once her mother's.

Nic had made their bed on a soft bed of leaves, gathered when she tended the horses. Morgan debated as he reclined there on his side, propped up on his elbow, his hand extended upward in invitation. "Come, Morgan. I don't usually bite," he teased. He saw her hesitation. "Soldiers often join their sleeping rolls together." That wasn't usually the case, but it was the best he could come up with. "It's not a sign of weakness but done out of need."

She still didn't move.

"Be reasonable. We need to get as much rest as possible. First light will be here before we know it, and tomorrow we need to put as much distance between them and us as possible. Trust me. I'm not the enemy. Let me keep you warm."

He watched her inch forward like a wild thing trying to make up its mind to bolt or to take the gift he offered. She cautiously lowered herself to the ground. Then in a gesture that surprised him, she offered part of her blanket.

"Nay, thank you. Wrap yourself in it. It's going to be a cold one," he said, glancing up again at the cloudless sky, broken only by the rising moon.

She settled down on the soft earth, turning her back to him and using her arm as a pillow. He did the same, allowing her to feel some privacy.

He waited to hear her breathing signal her surrender to sleep. He had asked her to trust him and she had. Only those who trust can sleep in the presence of danger. His very fiber spoke of her life being at risk. Yet, she had given in to sleep, the most vulnerable of positions. He rolled over to face her before taking his own blanket and spreading it over both of them.

As the moon came and went, the temperature dropped. It was a bone-chilling cold even for him, and he was certainly more prepared and acclimated to these conditions. Carefully gathering her in his arms, he brought her closer to his side. As he pulled her into the curve of his body, she settled in. It was like finding the right key to a lock and the two individual pieces effortlessly coming together.

Chapter 8

Sometime later, Nic stretched, looking up at the heavens, wondering why fate had placed this woman in his path. His friend Connor once told him years ago that if he thought fate was a crafty witch, then he was really going to love her sister destiny. Connor was right about fate. Nic had yet to meet her sister.

Morgan was just another burden as far as he was concerned. He really didn't want a wife. All he wanted was to serve his king. Noble and corny as it sounded, it was the truth. Having a wife would require more than he was willing to give by dividing his loyalties between a wife and King Henry. He really didn't want the distraction, either. All he had planned to do was to marry her and leave her at Seabridge. Now, that was unthinkable. Nevertheless, his own lands were in dire need of attention; he needed to go home. Morgan just complicated things.

My own lands. It was a foreign thought.

Brandon, his older brother, had taken responsibility for running the family lands after their father had become too frail to continue to be overlord. It was Brandon's birthright. Yet, his father's steward had dispatched an urgent summons, requesting that he return to his ancestral home of Heather Park, and it had taken nearly half a year for the message to catch up with him, moving as often as he did.

He hadn't been back in ages.

How many years had it been? Nic wondered. Eight or was it nine years now? How many sieges past? How many battles won or lost? And how many nights just like this, sleeping under the heavens? Far more than Nic could remember. He had stopped counting years ago.

Now, his father still breathed when his brother was long cold and dead in his grave. Brandon had died the previous winter of a wasting disease, and his brother had

55

left no children or wife, which apparently prompted King Henry's decree that he marry the Duchess of Seabridge.

Nic remembered vividly his conversation with Henry.

"Nic, my good man, you now have need of a suitable wife. I have left you to your own devices all these years, and in truth, it suited my purposes. However, the time has come to leave your selfish wishes behind."

"I'm still quite happy to be selfish, sire," he had said in all honesty.

"Well, my queen is right. It's time that you get married and settle down. It's up to you to pass the lineage on for future generations of loyal subjects to the crown."

"So, you want me to marry, settle, and have bairns? A tall order don't you think?" Nic teased. Until that moment, he had never given children a thought. There was still his youngest brother to carry on the family name. Cullen was a favorite of the ladies and would make a suitable husband and father.

"I have just the lady in mind for you. A true prize if she looks anything like her mother," the king had said good-naturedly with a wink and hearty slap on the back.

A prize? Hmm, maybe? Then again, maybe nay so much, Nic thought as his mind came back to the present.

He could barely make out Morgan's profile in the darkness.

Either way it didn't matter. Henry had spoken, so "that-is-that," as Henry was known to say. Nic shrugged. He would just adjust and alter his strategy as any good soldier does when faced with the failure of the first plan.

Turning his mind to other things, Nic needed to be moving north not east. London wasn't exactly where he thought he would end the month of April. Then again not much else was going according to plan. He wondered just how angry Henry was going to be. He certainly wasn't going to be pleased, but there was no way around it.

At least he was bringing his bride back with him to London. That was something, at least. They could have a hasty exchange of vows with the king and Queen Elizabeth as witnesses. What girl wouldn't want that?

Then he would leave her there in Henry's care as a lady-in-waiting to the queen. By doing that, Nic could meet his duty to his king and his father. Morgan would be safe in London with the queen. Henry would see to it. Then he could make his way back home.

"Well, damn," he mumbled. "So, much for my first plan," he said, realizing it solved some of his dilemma, but not all.

There was still the huge piece of rock left to conquer. The claim of Seabridge would be left unaccomplished even if the duchess were in the king's care. It would be paramount that he be there in person to do the claiming. He didn't see Lester going quietly.

Morgan interrupted his thoughts as she began to shiver, and she turned into his body for the warmth he could give her. He knew she was unaware of her movements. As Nic gathered her close, he mused he would have to see to a bath for her if he was to continue being in close quarters with her. She deserved to be fresh and clean after the spill into the bog along the side of that road. Even if she wasn't clean at the moment, she smelled feminine and her curves were a nice complement to her pretty smile.

It was a pleasant thought to drift off to sleep to.

~*****~

As the stars journeyed across the night sky, Morgan thrashed violently, jolting Nic from sleep. He felt her silent screams.

"It's all right. Easy, Morgan, easy. It's only a nightmare. Easy, lass."

Morgan instinctively stilled at the sound of his soothing voice. In her small and sleep-filled voice, Nic heard her as she drifted back into sleep.

"Da, I have missed you."

Nic found this startling. So, she could speak. More disturbing was her pathetic declaration of missing her father. It touched him deeply and unexpectedly.

He knew the story of the death of her entire family in one fatal blow. He would hold her if it gave her peace, even if it was only in her sleep.

As night gave way to the rose-colored fingers of first light, Nic eased Morgan out of his arms. She unconsciously protested the loss of his warmth. Nonetheless, they had overstayed, and this placed them in a vulnerable position. Nic sensed that Morgan waking up in his arms wouldn't be to his best advantage, regardless of how good the warmth might feel to him. He had no delusions after last evening of what her feelings were for him, but today was a new day and he was just beginning to make forward progress with her.

He was beginning to have a better understanding of his runaway bride. She was smart.

That much he was beginning to see.

Chapter 9

"Wake up, Morgan." Nic nudged her with the toe of his boot. "It's time to break camp. Hurry, now. We must make good time today if we're to arrive at The King's Court by nightfall." The King's Court was a small roadside inn known for hospitality and discretion. And Nic was in need of both.

At the prodding, Morgan rolled over, moaning from her aches and pains. Nic was correct. She was sore due to her fall, the cold night, and sleeping on unforgiving ground. Even her old dirty cot in the tower had some cushion against the stone floor. Not sure if she could get up without help, she tentatively sat up and began to stretch her protesting limbs.

In the early morning light, Nic noticed the evidence of her close call with death. Her lips were blue from the early morning cold, and she had a very nasty bruise on the left temple. He was thankful the fall hadn't killed her. That didn't negate the fact that they couldn't linger.

"I won't say it again, up now, and hurry. I've already broken my fast and watered the horses. We're just waiting on you to bundle your belongings, and then we can head out. You can eat as we go."

She nodded, getting up quickly.

"Your cloak, Morgan, pack it. It looks too much like a woman's garment." He really couldn't afford to have someone recognize her. "Here, take this." He tossed her an extra woolen shirt from his pack. "Put it on if you need the added warmth."

He stifled a laugh when she pulled the shirt on over her head. The sleeves went to her knees and the tail hit her midthigh. She flopped the arms around several times until her hands finally appeared. She was giggling at how absurd she must look.

"Let me know if you need more," Nic offered as he mounted Trojan.

She nodded, thankful for his guidance and his thoughtfulness.

She followed his lead. Obviously knowing where he was heading, Morgan remembered the day before him saying something about going to the king's court. That was excellent news to her, considering the alternative. Feeling her spirits rise, Morgan was certain this would work out after all.

Putting her trust in fate and her mother's words, Morgan settled in for whatever the day was to bring.

~*****~

As they mounted up and headed east, the stallion demanded her full and undivided attention. This gave Nic the opportunity to watch her without her being aware of his scrutiny. He was coming to some conclusions.

The first conclusion was he actually liked her.

Her short hair was almost a riot of curls from the damp and the lack of a brush. Nevertheless, somehow it wasn't unattractive. She was tall. Not that it mattered. He was a massive man, and his height of six feet seven inches always left him with women a great deal shorter, sometimes uncomfortably so. However, she was very slender and that was somewhat alarming to him. Normally, he liked his women soft and plump, to leave no doubt he was bedding a woman. Morgan, on the other hand, was passing nicely for a teenage boy. She was six feet tall, and in his opinion, she didn't have enough weight on her bones to sustain her. He wondered if she might be ill, yet she seemed healthy. He guessed time would tell on that point, too.

Morgan reminded him of a colt, all legs. At least she wasn't a mute, but he had no other way to discover if she was of normal intelligence. In time, he supposed. He needed to have a wife who could stimulate his mind, as well as his body. He knew she could speak, though he wasn't ready to tip his hand. As a result, the judgment would just have to remain undecided until he could engage her in conversation. He was also looking for an honest woman. In his experience, most women of nobility were not forthright. Morgan, at this point, was no exception.

She had lied to him and was still lying to him. In her defense, he understood her motivation, even if he didn't know the whole story or all the sordid details. He might have done the same if he were a woman and found himself in similar circumstances.

He felt sure there must be a good reason for the duchess to run and take on a disguise. He would get those details soon because his having those details were paramount in keeping her alive. He had no doubt that her instincts to survive were strong, and those same instincts obviously served her well to this point. He didn't take the lack of trust personally. *She is wary of me, and well she should be*, he acknowledged inwardly. He was a stranger to her and he wouldn't discourage Morgan's behavior until he could prove he wasn't going to harm her in any way. It would take some time for her to see him in his true light.

He wasn't perfect, but he was a good man with nothing except honorable intentions toward her. He would never knowingly harm her, and she would see that at some point. She was his woman and would eventually be the mother of his children. He would protect her and his future children with his life. No harm would come to her, at least not from his quarter. Furthermore, just because he didn't want to marry her, that didn't translate into him taking his frustrations out on her. Henry's displeasure was enough to prevent it, even if his own honor didn't dictate it.

"Demon, you're a beast," Morgan mumbled, breaking through his thoughts. Nic could see that she was having a devil of a time in her attempts to keep the horse out of the brambles and herself on his back.

Another issue, he thought with a sigh.

He needed to get her another horse before this one stopped allowing her to control him, and that was exactly what was going on between those two. The horse was just docile enough to allow her to keep her seat.

Not for the first time, he wondered exactly where she picked up this beast. Had there been a choice in taking the horse versus another? Nic was beginning to think not. He had also changed his opinion of the horse. At first, he thought the magnificent animal untrained and unruly. Now, he knew Morgan was simply an inexperienced rider. So much so, it surprised Nic that she even knew which end of the horse she was supposed to face.

The fact the horse was too much animal for her was only one reason why he needed to get her a different mount. They could ill afford for her to take another tumble from its back. Furthermore, this horse would just draw too much attention to them.

"Come, Morgan. Let us get off this road." He grabbed the reins of her horse and led her farther into the woods off the main road.

Nic dismounted and walked up beside her. "Come down off that brute." He waved her down, then held up his hand to help her dismount.

She refused his offer of help, sliding off Demon's wide back and falling flat on her rump on the leaf-covered forest floor. Nic turned away from her before she could see him smile.

Stubborn wench, he thought. But he admired her spirit of independence.

"Morgan, now that we're close to Bristol, I need to trade your mount and get one more suitable for you. I need you to stay behind while I do it."

Nic saw her expression. Crossing her arms over her chest, she looked at him speculatively.

"It'll be less noticeable if a knight rides in on a horse like yours. And I think we both can agree that being noticed is something neither one of us wants or needs with the search party still in the area. You know it's best."

Morgan still looked suspicious. Nic sighed heavily. He really didn't have time to debate his position on this.

"You trusted me last night to guard your very existence. Now, you don't trust me with the exchange of your horse?" Nic questioned. "Are you afraid I'll take him and not come back?" He felt perhaps that was exactly what she was thinking. He paused as if he expected her to answer the question. Morgan only stared.

What am I in truth afraid of? she wondered. His stealing her horse wasn't it; she decided that rather quickly. If that were his intention, he would have had plenty of time to steal her horse that morning while she slept. It was something else that nagged her.

"If it makes you feel better and gives you a feeling of security, I'll leave you Trojan. I can assure you his worth far exceeds this animal's value. He's a trained warhorse, and I don't have to tell you a man in my profession values his horse as much as his own life. Don't think for one moment I would leave him behind. I might leave you behind, but never him," he teased.

She found no humor in what he said and stayed silent. His leaving her was what she feared. He saw that clearly.

So did she.

He allayed her fears. "I promise, I'm not abandoning you, Morgan. Stay here out of sight and stay as quiet as possible. I'll be gone much of the day. On my honor, I'll try to be back at the latest by midafternoon."

Morgan didn't know what to feel. She would be totally defenseless and alone. He was correct, however, so she would remain behind.

"It's obvious that we cannot go to Seabridge, so I'll bring back enough supplies to get us to London."

Morgan nodded yet was uncertain.

Nic cupped her shoulder and lightly squeezed it, offering reassurance. "I'll come back, Morgan. You have my word as a king's man. In the meantime, you're not to leave the area. Stay put, you hear me?" He shook his finger for emphasis. "That's an order and not a request. Do you understand?" He waited for her to acknowledge him. "Good, and use this if you have to," he said as he shoved a mean-looking knife into her hands.

He was no longer jesting and his command was serious. Her safety depended on her following his order and staying put. He had to trust her as much as she did him.

Nic gracefully swung up onto Demon's back, the beast protesting to the added weight of the unfamiliar rider. As Demon settled, bowing to the Nic's superior skills, Nic paused to give Morgan an opportunity to protest. Instead, she awarded him with a single nod of consent and a small uncertain wave of goodbye. Wheeling Demon around without a backward glance, he headed back to the main road and into the late morning sun.

~*****~

"What's taking that man so long?" Morgan wondered aloud.

She could have bartered a dozen horses, secured all the necessary supplies to support a yearlong siege, and baked bread in the time it was taking him.

Morgan was growing restless. *Not always a good thing*, she thought. Her apprehension was a big part of that restlessness. She was alone but that didn't bother her. It was a natural state. Yet, somehow this time it felt different, and she was growing concerned for Nic's safety. It never occurred to her that she was in any danger.

Nic's company wasn't so bad now that she was beginning to become accustomed to him. As long as she kept her distance, thinking of him as protection, she was in truth very comfortable. Only when she thought of him as a man did her uneasiness resurface, and that wasn't because she felt he would abuse her. She was his responsibility, and she knew he would take that responsibility seriously.

They had ridden in silence, talking little. Well, she was supposed to be mute after all, and he was a man of few words and even fewer words spoken about himself. She knew that he was extremely confident in who he was as a man and a soldier. That being the case, he probably didn't feel the need to secure her approval or impress her. She was his squire, and even if he treated her with respect, she was still no one of importance.

Most everything Morgan knew of Nic was what he had shared the first day. He was from the far north of England, and she would have picked that up from his accent. His burr was unmistakably a result of his roots in the wild Scottish Highlands and hanging around King Henry's men. It was a mashed-up mix that she at times struggled to understand. He told her he was heading north after he finished taking care of some business at Seabridge. That corresponded with his accent. She knew it was nasty business, but obviously, it wasn't urgent business or currently they wouldn't be heading back to London.

She knew he was King Henry's knight and in high standing. No doubts there.

"That is obvious," she said to Trojan as they walked in the woods together.

Morgan had watched him practice the previous day prior to turning in for the evening. With his fighting skill, she could see him being high on King Henry's list of favorites. With his dark good looks, it wouldn't surprise her if he were a top favorite of the ladies, too. He was one of the most devastatingly handsome men she had ever seen, which was even more reason for her to keep her distance. Her survival instincts were telling her to stay close enough for the protection that he was offering but to preserve enough distance between them to never touch.

Coming back to her surroundings and out of her thoughts, Morgan realized she had wandered away from the clearing where Nic had left her with clear instructions to stay put. Thank heavens she had brought Nic's prized horse with her.

"Leave me behind, but not his horse." She made a most undignified sound at her mental musings of Nic and what he could do with his horse. "Although he is beautiful," Morgan said as she patted the beast, lovingly running her hand over his neck. "You, not him."

She cleared up that distinction in her mind. Trojan snorted.

"Oh, all right. I confess. Nic is, too," she said as Trojan nudged her arm, as if calling her bluff. "I always was a bad liar. There, happy now?" Trojan bobbed his head.

Morgan continued to wander, seeing no harm in it. The day was mild and there was no one in sight.

After an hour, Morgan had to admit she was lost.

"Oh boy, Trojan, Nic is going to be pretty upset if he returns and finds you gone," she said, stroking his velvety nose. Trojan bobbed his head in agreement. "Can you back me up that this was really not intentional?"

Just as if he understood her, he shook his head setting his bridle to jingling.

"Nay, huh? Will you not reconsider?" Morgan asked as she hugged his neck in comfort.

He pawed at the ground once as if to put his foot down. Maybe he did understand more than she thought?

"Well, see if I pull the burs out of that tail of yours ever again."

Trojan blew softly.

"Right, I just confessed that I'm a bad liar. Very well, fine. So, I'll pick the burs, but you have to confess that Nic's concern and affection for you are almost unnatural."

The horse was the man's main concern, she was certain, and she couldn't blame him. Trojan was a fine piece of horseflesh and critical for his chosen profession. This lovely animal was gentle when necessary, but he would tear your face off if the need presented itself. That training was reserved for only the finest, and she would love to breed him to some of her stable stock. The outcome would be fantastic.

Taking a deep breath, she reasoned that she had time to find her way back.

After another half hour, she was more than a little nervous. She was walking in circles, remembering that same fallen log from an hour past.

"Oh, aye, I should have listened."

Why had she not listened to him? Taking a couple deep breaths to calm her heart, Morgan looked around to take her bearings. She had remembered the morning sun rising to her back as she set off in search of the roots and berries she had bundled in her shirttail.

She needed to be back before Nic even knew she had wandered off.

"There's time, right, boy?"

Trojan bobbed his head in agreement just as if he understood her.

"Now, who's the bad liar?"

Chapter 10

"Damn it, Morgan!"

Little did she know that Nic was already aware of her little disobedience and was oscillating between frantic and furious. Where could she have wandered off? Fearful to call out, Nic kept his control. If the search party had not cleared the area, and he suspected they hadn't, he could place her into greater danger.

Nic knew from the news in the town tavern that the party sent by Lord Brentwood had just left the inn that morning. The best he could discover from the information he gathered was they were continuing to head east. The word was they were looking for the Duchess of Seabridge, and there was a sizable reward for her return.

What worried Nic most was the lack of stipulation of her condition upon return; she only needed to be alive. That said a great deal to him about the uncle who was claiming to want her back. Not to place stipulations on her condition of return all but insured she might come back but not necessarily in one piece, or unsullied.

The claim was that unknown assailants had kidnapped her, plucking her from the tender arms of her distraught and loving uncle. He guessed it would never do for word to get out that Morgan was running of her own free will.

Nic smiled despite himself. It had been a smart move on Morgan's part to dress the part of a young boy. What surprised him was her age. She was twenty, not looking a day over fifteen.

"Where is she," he cursed silently, continuing to track her and wondering how in heaven and hell one slip of a girl could be so much trouble.

"And, by God, where is my horse!" he cursed her further for not following his instructions.

Thankful for the distinctive pattern of the shoe Trojan was wearing, he finally picked up the tracks, all the while telling himself that she was fine and it would just be a matter of minutes before he found her. Nic was fighting a rising concern, a feeling foreign to him. *Surely, it is just fear and concern of losing my horse*, he reasoned.

~*****~

Meanwhile, Morgan was more confident. She knew where she was and continued her trek back toward the clearing. As she walked, she picked early-ripened nuts and berries along the way. Finding her way again relieved her of the fear of being lost and allowed her to become so absorbed in the day and the beauty of the forest that she didn't hear the noise behind her.

Once she did there wasn't time to react.

The men were on her before she could scream, and one of them placed a filthy hand over her mouth and nose. Holding his blade tightly to her throat, his rank mouth, full of rotting teeth, hovered only inches from her own. She gagged from his breath.

Oh, yes, she should have listened to Nic.

They're going to steal his horse and then Nic is going to kill me for sure, she thought.

It never occurred to her these three men might save him the trouble.

Morgan heard a sharp whistle. And then she heard one of the men scream in pain as Trojan reared and came down sharply, ripping his face off and stomping him repeatedly. Trojan reared again, his hooves flailing at the second man foolish enough to try and steal him. Neither of the two remaining men gave the dead man any attention. And, by some miracle, the man got Trojan calm enough to grab his bridle.

" 'Ey, Gunter, look what we 'ave 'ere. It must be our lucky day, ol' boy. We just found us a fine piece of 'orseflesh and a sweet young boy to boot. I found 'im so, I get 'im first."

His partner grunted a reply and began to go through Nic's bags, having somehow calmed Trojan to the point of being docile. He wasn't looking at her, the dead man to his left, or her assailant.

The man holding her squeezed her tighter, pulling the back of the blade lightly across her skin. "Open your mouth and make one sound, and I'll cut your bloody throat, I will. Be a good boy and it will be over quickly."

Realization dawned on her, and Morgan began to fight in earnest, realizing his intention was to rape her, even though they thought she was a boy. She wasn't about to let that happen and certainly not without a fight. She hadn't managed to escape her uncle just to die in some forest at the hands of this moat scum.

Suddenly, Morgan felt her attacker go limp as his body toppled and pinned her under the dead weight. She heard Nic's voice through the haze and the pounding of her blood coursing through the veins.

"Continue to touch what belongs to me, and you will die. Just ask either of your friends."

The statement delivered with no inflection left little doubt in the mind of the would-be thief. This boy wasn't worth the wrath of a full-blown knight; the horse was another story. In a split second, the thug weighed it out and felt the horse wasn't worth the trouble, either. He dropped the reins of the warhorse and ran.

"Smart man," Nic said as he watched the thief run back toward town.

"Morgan, are you harmed?" Nic rolled the filthy dead man off Morgan and saw what she had yet to feel. "Oh, sweet mother of God!"

The blade must have cut her as the man fell. To him, Morgan looked to be losing blood.

Feeling the weight lifted from her, Morgan began to kick and claw her way past the dead body. Once she was free on her feet, she kicked him repeatedly before Nic could pull her away.

"Morgan, stop! He's dead! Easy, easy," Nic said as she began to fight him. "Easy. Just breathe."

Once Morgan realized it was Nic, she collapsed against him in an adrenaline crash. "Oh, God, he was going to rape me." Her words were muffled into his chest as her knees gave way.

Nic wasn't about to tell her that after the man raped her he would have killed her.

Cursing himself, he wondered what the devil he could possibly have been thinking to leave her alone. He should have protected her. There was blood everywhere. He picked her up as if she were a rag doll weighing less than his saddle blanket and took her a few feet away from the filthy corpse. Gently, he set her down on the ground, knowing she was in shock. She would feel the pain soon enough as he began to search for the potentially fatal wounds. Discovering the mashed berries in her shirt, Nic realized she was unhurt and just covered in juice.

His concern turned to frustration for her disobeying a direct order.

"What were you thinking?" Nic yelled. And that was just the beginning. He was fierce in his tirade, and Morgan closed down, having no way of knowing that this was his standard release valve after battle. The reaction wasn't very pretty, but it was effective in releasing any unused energy not spent on an enemy.

He ran his hand through his hair in a gesture of frustration, turning his back to her. He hung his head in an effort to collect himself and regain control. Then realization struck him full force.

"Oh, God, she could have died," he murmured, in stark contrast to the rest of his monologue. He turned around to face her. "Morgan, those men not only would have raped you but would have killed you after." His heart softened, and he got down on one knee. "Morgan, look at me, lass."

She didn't hear him and her eyes were vacant, her mind having fled to a safer place. It was a safety mechanism perfected over the years and one Nic had seen often in the untrained soldiers who were in the grip of shock and denial.

Again he demanded, "Look at me!" he said forcefully, pulling her back to him.

She finally blinked and raised her eyes to meet his, beginning to hear his words through the haze of the aftermath.

"You're mine to protect. Don't think for one minute to ever defy me again, or I'll be forced to punish you, lad."

He said it knowing he didn't mean it. She took the flats of her hands and pushed him away, scrambling back to her feet.

"Go to hell, you sorry bastard!" Morgan said, coming back to reality quickly. She wasn't taking that from him or anyone else ever again. Morgan didn't realize she had spoken as she stomped off to find her new horse.

He sighed heavily, following close behind. "Morgan, I'm verray sorry. I did not mean that. I wouldn't hurt you. I promise, Morgan, on my honor. But why could you not do as I asked? Not even for a few hours? All I asked of you was to stay put." She looked at him, not knowing what to feel. "They nearly killed you and almost stole my horse."

Nic looked at Morgan, knowing had they succeeded on either count, it would have been, indeed, a tragedy.

He turned to go recover the other object of his affection.

Chapter 11

Morgan barely noticed the scenery as they continued to fly over the countryside. She had not put up a fight as Nic placed her behind him on Trojan.

He had picked up two horses in exchange for Demon. In her mind, that wasn't a fair trade. She decided not to argue. She had agreed, and an agreement was her word. Her newly acquired mount, which she would soon ride, was pure white and aptly named Salt. The docile and easygoing bay's name was Vernon.

Both horses trotted behind them, their reins tied to Trojan. Nic had securely tied all their supplies to the horses' backs.

All right, she thought, *so he got two horses and food.* Maybe it was a decent trade, especially if she could talk him into letting her have Trojan for stud a time or two. She would have to ask when the time was right.

Nic hadn't spoken two words since they had mounted up and headed east after her near rape in the woods. That was just fine with her.

Her shock had given way to anger, and anger eventually to pensiveness.

She wondered what drove a man like Nic McKinnon, realizing again that she knew nothing about him. The fact that she wanted to know more was a surprise. Where was home for him? Did he have family? Where had his travels taken him? What was his business at Seabridge? Her mind continued to reel, understanding it was just morbid curiosity driving her. She was no longer upset with him, having already forgiven him for his threat of beating her within an inch of her life. Things said in the heat of battle, and their encounter could certainly fall in that category, should not be held against someone.

She let it go.

However, what she couldn't let go was the call of nature.

She loathed asking him to stop. Nevertheless, her discomfort was just about at critical levels as she tapped him on the shoulder and pointed to the woods.

He stopped. What else could he do?

She wasn't sure if it was for her benefit or the horses, but she slid from the horse and headed for the trees.

~*****~

"I had hoped to give you the luxury of a bath this evening, but because of our encounter earlier today and the time it cost us, we'll not make The King's Court by nightfall unless we ride our horses until they drop," he said as she reappeared.

"Well, as lovely as a bath would be, my lord, it's surely not worth placing unwarranted stress on the horses," she said without thinking.

It was then Morgan realized she had spoken, and her hand involuntarily flew to cover her mouth. No shoving those words back in where they came from, she rightfully reasoned. And now he knew she wasn't mute.

She looked into Nic's eyes, and their gazes locked. She heard him laugh softly.

He had known, but how could he? Then she remembered her telling him to go to hell.

"So I see the cat's no longer got your tongue." Nic went on before she could comment. "We'll bed down here for the night," he said as he began to unload the horses of the necessary supplies that they would need for the night. "It seems a good spot, and I believe there's a pool of water close. Take the horses there, Morgan."

Again, it was a beautiful place. Trees on three sides ringed the open area and large, ancient boulders dotted the new spring grass carpeting the clearing. The sunset presented a beautiful display of orange tinged with pink and deeper shades of red. Morgan felt this time of day had a peace all its own, a finality of a sorts. As if to promise that sleep would come and bring peace.

Morgan waited for the horses to drink their fill. The pond wasn't large, but it did have clean and clear spring-fed waters. That cleansing water called to her with an invitation too promising and strong to resist. The late afternoon was still warm, and she felt filthy. She smelled of him, of blood, of death, and she smelled of something more primal: her own fear.

The need to wash and be clean overwhelmed her as she stood there.

After securing the horses, Morgan tore her clothes off, not caring that the action was destroying them. That was done with full intent. She would never wear them again. Quickly stripping down and moving to the horses, she reached into the saddlebag to pull out the bar of precious hand-milled soap that she found one night while exploring her mother's old rooms. She clutched it to her and closed her eyes as she remembered the night she first discovered the treasure and how she had hidden it away from her uncle for fear he would take it from her. Sometimes, she would pull the bar out just to smell it, and then her mother's face would swim before her mind's eye. The soap's sweet aroma was fading with time along with her memories of her mother's young and beautiful face.

All this is Lester's fault, she thought. He was really the bastard in this circumstance and not Nic. Her losing her memories and her faltering faith was squarely on her uncle's shoulders. He could take her physical wealth, but he was never going to take her spirit.

"Keep the faith, heart of my heart." The soft voice whispered in her mind just before Morgan opened her eyes. "It's hard, Mamma, but I'll try," she promised softly.

Knowing time was short, Morgan walked into the cool waters beckoning her. Dipping beneath the shimmering surface, she allowed the water to caress her just as it had when she was a child. She reemerged on the opposite bank, then dipped back under to return to the bank closest to the horses.

Morgan emerged out of the cleansing waters, feeling reborn as a stronger woman for what had happened. She survived. She would continue to survive. She was Morgan Pembridge, Seventh Duchess of Seabridge, a descendent of the mighty and fearless Viking people. More importantly, she was her mother's daughter.

After dressing in what was now the only set of clothing she owned, she took the filthy clothes and tucked them into a hollowed log. She didn't want to leave any evidence of their presence just in case the search party was behind them, but she never wanted to look at those clothes again. They would only serve to remind her of what almost happened.

It was her fault. She had disobeyed an order.

She vowed the event would never be repeated. She would depend on Nic's authority. He would see to her survival as long as she trusted him with her life. Could she really do that?

Somehow, it just felt right.

She would keep the faith, and tomorrow was a new day.

But today there was still something she needed to do.

~*****~

Hurrying back to camp, Morgan tried to formulate in her mind an apology for her disobedience. "I'm sorry, Nic," just didn't seem adequate.

She saw him waiting. Having taken up a watchful position at the edge of the camp, he was casually leaning against a tree, his booted foot drawn up to rest on the trunk. His shirt's unbound laces left it open at the neck, revealing more skin on a man than she had ever seen. She forced herself not to stare. That would be rude. But she couldn't look away to save her life. His allure was so strong, and there was an air of danger and sensuality clinging to him. Struck once more at how beautiful he was, Morgan quickly brought her gaze back to his face to see him smugly smiling, one eyebrow raised.

Nic pushed off the tree, before dropping the blade of grass he had been running through his fingers. "Well, I see you found the pool and made good use of it. Lucky for us, we didn't need The King's Court after all for that bath." Nic pulled his shirt over his head and handed it to her. "Be a good lad and see what you can do with this and when you're done lay out our supper while I go bathe."

"I think I can save it," she said to cover her misstep of openly appraising him.

"Aye, well just do your best. 'Tis all I ask of any task you do for me."

He was warming to the idea of his spirited, if unconventional, bride. On his way to the spring-fed pool, Nic pondered the transformation the bath had brought in her. Free of grime, her face was nothing short of beautiful, but not in a classical way. Although her coloring was wrong to be considered fashionable, and she was much too tall, her hair much too short, and her body much too thin for the current standard of beauty, she was beautiful in a way that held his interest all the same. Nic was never one to hold to fashion in his clothes or in his women. And she was his woman for better or worse by the king's decree.

He had to hand it to her because she had not fallen apart today. Most women he knew would have been in hysterics. She did have spirit and fortitude, and that was something even many seasoned men lacked. He smiled, thinking about the way she had cursed the corpse of her attacker. Quite colorful and imaginative, he admitted with a smile.

Nic swam several laps across the shallow pool. It felt good to have some exercise, even if it wasn't nearly enough. He was accustomed to more physically intense activity than he was getting, and it was beginning to make him edgy. That edginess wasn't in the favor of his current traveling companion.

After completing his bath, he returned to the camp to find Morgan performing the duties as his squire. She had gathered firewood, made the sleeping pallets, and laid out a fresh shirt, alongside the meats and bread for dinner.

Sitting next to each other and leaning up against a fallen log, they shared sips of the mulled wine from the skin and ate in silence. Nic knew that she feared that any moment the questions would start. He also knew there would be no appeasing him once they did. So, he did not ask. Instead, Nic had waited for her to talk. He hadn't pressured her. Morgan was still shaken and he understood the day was traumatic enough and wouldn't add to it. So, they sat in companionable silence, looking into the fire.

"It's been a long day," Nic declared as he placed the wineskin back into the pack, doused the fire, and gestured for her to follow suit as he covered himself with his blanket. She had retrieved her cloak and blanket from her saddlebag earlier, so she rolled up in them and bedded down for the night. Turning her back to Nic, she stared into the low glowing ashes and sighed, fidgeting to find a comfortable position. Nic smiled. He could see the point. Morgan had not done as good a job of the underbedding as he had done the night before. It was lumpy, but it would have to do. Considering it was her first attempt he would hold his tongue and give her opportunity to better her skills as the days progressed. Finally finding a passable spot, Nic could tell that Morgan was beginning to relax but he could tell that she was still awake. He didn't turn away from her as he had the night before but instead lay on his back, cushioning his head on his forearms and looked up at the stars.

Sometime later, a small, barely discernible voice broke his thoughts.

"I'm sorry," she offered.

Nic couldn't help but smile. *She simply cannot be silent; after all, she is a woman,* he thought with some mirth.

"I've already let it go, Morgan. You should, too."

"I shall try," she said after a few minutes. "Good night, Sir Nic."

"Good night, Morgan," he said softly, matching her tone.

Then, as the night's silence stretched on, the small voice intruded into his thoughts again.

"Sir Nic?" Morgan quietly asked just in case he was sleeping.

"Aye, Morgan?"

"I know I'm not your horse, but thank you for being there for me today."

In that instant, whether realizing it or not, he had just lost the first battle of his life, feeling the fissures begin to break the ice around his heart.

Chapter 12

Nic waited for the steady rhythm of her breathing to signal she had fallen into a deeper sleep.

Gathering her to him, he wondered how holding her could feel so right. She fit so perfectly in the curve of his arms. With each breath he took, he inhaled the feminine smell of the soap she used to bathe. It haunted him as they had sat in silence that evening by the fire.

Lavender and vanilla...

Not many women wore the scent. It was very expensive and even fewer could wear it with success. On her it was subtle, mixing with her unique scent, working well with her natural body chemistry.

He placed his chin on top of her head, rubbing his cheek to her hair. He had noticed how her hair looked soft and silky with just a touch of wave to it. As Nic brushed his lips against the baby-fine hair, thoughts came unbidden of how her hair must have looked before she cut it. Long, dark, and wrapped around him as they slept intertwined.

He remembered how she looked that afternoon as she bathed. He had followed her to be sure she wasn't going to run. Unlike tonight, he was still uncertain of her intent, and she had all the horses packed with enough supplies to last her days should she decide to make a break. Standing there watching her, he had known the moment she had decided to take a bath. He had seen her expression of longing as she stood by the pool's edge. He knew he should have gone back to camp to give her privacy, yet he needed to be sure she was going to be all right and that no one else was a threat to her.

She had torn her clothes from her body, uncaring that she was turning them into rags. It touched his heart to hear the sounds of anger and impotent rage coming from her as she stripped the garments away. She threw them to the ground, as if they represented something more foul than what they were, and he watched as she stomped on them in fury and frustration. He had known in that instant she was remembering the earlier attack and maybe something more. Worried for her, he stayed and was beginning to see that under her shell of control was a fragile woman, but a woman with a strong spirit, too. She was going to be fine given time and an environment where she could thrive. She was a survivor and he respected her for that strong spirit.

He remembered his moments of indecision. If he went to her to give her comfort, then she would have known he had discovered her secret. If he did nothing, she would continue to carry the burden alone. He decided her secret needed to be maintained for just a little longer. He could always soothe her wounded spirit later. He knew things didn't go away that easily, no matter if he did insinuate she needed to let it go.

Lying there, Nic wondered why he even cared that she carried her anguish alone. He should not be worried if she hurt emotionally, but he did. That wasn't part of the responsibility of his position as her husband and protector. His responsibility was for her physical safety and well-being only. No one expected him to do more for his wife than to see to her safety and to give her children. Moreover, he dared anyone to doubt he would do his duty by her. He had no other choice as a knight of the realm and as her husband.

Morgan began to move in her sleep. Nic wondered what demons she harbored. Pulling her closer, he soothed her with soft words as he looked into her lovely face that was so trusting in sleep. Unconsciously moving to adjust her body against his, he brushed away the veil of silk from her cheek, feeling something deep inside him stir to life. His long dead heart began to beat.

"Be easy, my sweet. You're safe. I'll not let the monsters or dragons get you this night," he said while tenderly kissing the side of her forehead. "Or ever."

Strange that he should feel that to be a vow. He was beginning to discover he was also not without his demons to wrestle. As Morgan settled, her breathing became regular; Nic drifted into sleep, giving over to the effects of the warmth and rightness of Morgan's body pressed to his.

Chapter 13

Morgan woke with a start. The sun was shining, the early morning rays warming her face.

Where am I? she wondered.

As she sat up and blinked the fog of sleep from her eyes, she realized she was in the clearing. Looking around, she also realized she was alone.

Why would Nic leave her? Morgan knew he was really angry yesterday. She could sense it. But she had apologized for her disobedience and for the fact she had almost cost Nic his horse, but surely it didn't warrant desertion.

She didn't see him, the horses, or the supplies. She saw only a handkerchief holding a lump of cheese and the wineskin left by the cold ashes of last night's fire.

The bastard had left her there alone with no idea where she was and no way to protect herself. He took her mount and her supplies, and he'd left her here alone. Anger swept over her. She knew it was partly to cover her fears. Anger was an emotion she could better handle than the cold strangling grip of fear.

She stomped around the camp, jerking up her meager possessions. There wasn't much to collect. "And he has the nerve to accuse me of thievery?" she asked the field rabbit who had stopped his grazing close by to watch her. "I'll hunt him down, and I'll make him pay for this," she vowed.

"Perhaps, you'll allow me to join you in this manhunt? I've not run anyone through in a few hours."

Nic was quick to remove the amusement from his face once he saw that she was actually in distress, which was thinly veiled by anger. It shocked him a little that his perceived abandonment would affect her so. Did she think him so untrustworthy as to steal away from her like a thief in the night?

Morgan whirled at the smooth velvety voice behind her. She had not heard a sound until he spoke. Relief filled her, and she let that emotion show on her face.

What was also evident to Nic was that the relief Morgan felt was short-lived.

"Have the decency next time to tell me you're leaving!" she snapped.

"Why? To give you an opportunity to shoot an arrow into my back?" He raised one dark brow in amusement.

"Nay. I don't know how to shoot… yet," Morgan said as a catty little smile graced her lips, and it left Nic wondering if he was actually safe or not.

Nic saw the play of emotions across Morgan's face. He knew she had gone from relieved to angry in seconds and then to relieved again. So she had a temper when she felt threatened. Fight or flight? For her it would be a fight. He logged that as one more fact to remember about her.

She also had a sense of humor; he just had to keep trying to find it.

"Mount up. It's time for us to ride." Trojan danced sideways, eager to be on the road. Nic pulled him up beside Salt. "Let me give you two pieces of information about me, Morgan. First, don't question my honor when it comes to those I have promised to take into my care. If I leave you, it will be because you've asked me to go."

"Second?" she asked softly, realizing she had hit a nerve with him.

"Heed my advice. It would be in your best interest if you learn to curb that temper of yours. You may find it will get you into serious trouble one day. As my squire, I would find myself honor bound to come to your defense. And even if I'm a soldier by profession, I'm not one for taking a life for trivial reasons. That being said, if I find I must take a life on your behalf, I do strongly recommend you make it count. There may not be another in the offering."

With those words of advice, Nic turned Trojan around and headed east into the morning sun.

Chapter 14

"Bloody bad luck," Nic mumbled.

The run of good luck wasn't holding with the weather. They had enjoyed two days of mild weather for traveling, but now it was miserable. Rain had started falling softly on them shortly after they broke camp.

The rain had turned from inconvenient to uncomfortable and then to cold and dangerous. The misty drizzle quickly gave way to wind blowing heavy gray sheets of rain sideways, and the roadway was turned to muck and mire. The travel was treacherous at times, risking broken limbs of both horse and rider.

Water ran down Morgan's legs and into her shoes, filling them to the rim. Dumping the rain out was pointless. She had stopped trying hours ago, realizing it was more trouble than it was worth.

The rain soaking through her clothes, making them cling to her like a soggy second skin, was the least of her worries. The numbness she felt in her hands, feet, and backside were caused from equal parts unrelenting rain, cold weather, and the pace Nic had demanded they keep.

Never complaining, Morgan understood the need to place as much distance as possible between them and the search party that was scouring the countryside for the Duchess of Seabridge. She hoped the search party, being sane men, had stopped to find shelter from this God-awful weather, while Nic took the opportunity to gain some ground.

She hadn't escaped her uncle just to die of consumption brought on from having to sleep outside in rainy conditions. She hoped they would make the King's Court tonight, and if that meant they pushed hard, so be it.

With that mental decision made, she detached as she had done so naturally over the years when she was threatened or physically uncomfortable. Withdrawing from what would do her harm had become a defense mechanism. She retreated within.

~*****~

Morgan impressed Nic, and that wasn't something easily done.

He had driven them as if the devil and his minions were behind them. Frowning, Nic wasn't so sure that her uncle might not be the devil if half his reputation was true. At any rate, the pace was grueling, even for him. Morgan hadn't spoken a word of complaint. She was quiet, which was probably for the best. So, he left her to her own coping mechanism. He had seen this behavior before in battle when men had endured all they could take. Nic thought it best if she could continue the pace.

As the miles rolled past, he kept a close eye and felt he was between a rock and a very hard spot. He knew they needed to make it to The King's Court with all haste because of the weather. As tough as Morgan might actually be, she was still a woman and deserved better than a muddy bed on the side of the road.

Darkness came and without a light source, Nic couldn't see her face clearly. Still, he knew Morgan was about to drop from her saddle, judging from the sluggish and slumping outline of her body. He would have taken her up on his horse and settled her in front of him if they were not already so close to their destination.

He was exhausted. Hating to admit that condition didn't change the fact. The past two nights' sleep had been fitful because of Morgan. Furthermore, he hadn't gotten any sleep in the saddle with the need to skirt the search party during the day. Now the infernal weather was slowing them up, and the lack of sleep was beginning to wear on him. In spite of his reputation, he wasn't indestructible.

And if he was this miserable, he could only venture a guess what Morgan was experiencing. Soon he would try to make it up to her.

Nic was looking forward to a decent shelter for them for the night. What sane man wouldn't be? he questioned.

Nonetheless, there was still a catch. Originally, necessity dictated the deception Morgan had started. That necessity was still a driving factor, and he had to be sure to keep the facade going. So, like it or not, Morgan would continue to act as his squire, as long as the search party remained in the vicinity. They were too close for Nic's comfort, even though he was able to skirt them the first day and had been just in front of them or running parallel the last two days. If his instincts were correct, the search party would be at the inn tomorrow. He also felt sure they would stop and inquire because he would stop if he were in their position.

His guess was the search party was still looking for a woman and a black stallion. No one would take note of a lone knight and his skinny, young squire. Such happenings were commonplace throughout the countryside these days. However, the locals would quickly take notice of a lone knight and a young woman. The reward for the information was substantial and too inviting to expect them to keep her whereabouts a secret. He really couldn't blame the common folk for giving them up. With the astronomical reward Brentwood posted, a man could feed a large family for years. Times were hard for these country people. Food was precious and sometimes scarce.

The ruse must and would continue for Morgan's safety, which brought him to another dilemma. Squires usually slept in the outbuildings with the horses or in the common room on the floor, and as a rule, they didn't have sleeping quarters of their own. That being the case, Nic was certain he would have to see what he could do about getting Morgan into a secure and warm shelter, while at the same time not raising suspicions. Having her sleep in the common room wasn't even a consideration, and he would continue through the night before allowing her to sleep in the stables.

Nic wondered how Morgan was holding up. It was evident to him that she was having problems of her own. She looked beyond miserable and exhausted nearly to the point of falling out of her saddle as they slowly made their way up the muddy road approaching The King's Court. It had been dark for some time, and there was no way that Morgan would know where they were. Nic realized that he hadn't offered to tell her, and she hadn't asked. At this point, he figured that she was probably past caring and just wanted to get there with as little delay as possible. Nic was trying to accommodate.

Nic could see that Morgan was anxious. They were approaching civilization and this increased the risk of discovery. He hoped that she would shove her anxiety aside and trust his decision.

Besides, he could smell the smoke from a fire as it drifted along the breeze on the wet evening air. The smells of food were coming from where they would stop, and they could see the glow of the lights beckoning warmly, a beacon in the night's shadows. It was the sweet promise of warmth, food, and an end to the interminable jostling in the saddle that kept them going.

"The King's Court, indeed, pfftt," Morgan snorted as it came into view. She saw it wasn't King Henry's court at all, not by a long stretch. The King's Court was a small roadside inn.

"Did you say something?" Nic tossed over his shoulder through the darkness, knowing what had elicited her comment. He wanted to draw her out but couldn't see the look she gave him. *It is just as well. I can imagine,* he thought.

Nic hoped that the prospect of warm food, a warm bath, warm dry clothes, and a bed was too much of a promised reward for her to remain too vexed with him.

"Not exactly the king's court I had in mind," she said and recognized that this was just a slight delay in gaining her audience with the king. She would have her audience… eventually. Yet, with chagrin, she admitted it wouldn't be today. She shoved her disappointment aside. A bath sounded so much better.

Nic pulled Trojan up just enough to allow Morgan's horse to come alongside. He explained it wasn't routine for the squires to sleep in their own quarters in an inn but rather in the outbuildings with the horses. As she was his squire, this is where she would normally be required to sleep.

Morgan moaned with disappointment and hung her head. Her distress was obvious to him.

Nic reached across and lifted her chin with his finger. "However, for not complaining about our pace, which by the way was necessary in case you were wondering, I promise I'll do my best to get you inside. If not, we'll keep moving. If I can get you inside, I'll also try to get you a warm bath and dry clothes. Here is what we'll need to do…"

He quickly set the plan and was glad Morgan agreed with little dispute.

"Up you come." Nic pulled her into his lap on the saddle. He immediately noticed how slight she was in spite of her height. "Keep this cloak wrapped around you and keep your face turned into my neck."

Morgan did as she was told to do. Savoring the warmth coming from her body, Nic wondered why he had waited this long to hold her in his arms.

"Perfect. Now, don't talk under any circumstances. You're mute remember? Well, most of the time," he added under his breath.

95

She gave him a playful elbow in the ribs forcing his breath to rush out in the unexpected blow. It was far from damaging to his warrior physique, yet it was annoying all the same.

"Behave!" Nic ordered.

"You deserved that," she said, annoyed more with the weather and less with him. "Too bad, I can't punch the weather gods."

"Were that possible, you'd have to wait until I was done," Nic said, then laughed. He could see her point. "Take heart. We're almost there."

Nic spotted the young groom just yards ahead. "Ho there, lad. I need your help. My squire has taken a nasty spill from his horse. I'll pay you to tend the horses for me, and there'll be an extra coin or two if you watch them through the night."

"Aye, sir, it will be my pleasure," the boy said as he reached for the coin Nic extended.

"Good, then run inside and secure us a room. Ask the matron to begin water for a bath for me and dressings for my man. When you're finished taking care of that, come back to the stables. I'll get the rest of your coin at that point." He headed to the stables. It was never good to pay for all services in advance.

The boy ran into the warmth of the inn. Reemerging a few moments later, he gave them assurances the room was ready and the bath was coming up shortly.

Paying little heed to the other patrons seeking decent shelter from the elements, Nic carried Morgan into the inn through the common room and straight up the stairs. Given the number of people taking shelter, Nic was surprised they even had a room available. He suspected some poor soul had been turned out to place them. Money talked, and few could come up with the coin he just pressed into the innkeeper's hand.

The matron was aware of the fall of Nic's squire and inquired how she could be of assistance.

Nic declined, thanking her. He was accustomed to tending the minor wounds of his men and promised to call her if he needed further aid.

"I believe the bath and dressings will be good. I'd appreciate you securing a dry change of clothes for him. I'll pay for the garments."

"Nay, my lord, that will not be necessary. I'm sure ye will return them as soon as your squire's clothes dry by the fire." Taken by Nic's tall good looks, the matron of the inn blushed like a maiden when he smiled at her. "Anything else?" she offered, hoping for an extra coin for herself.

"My thanks, but that'll be sufficient," Nic said, then inclined his head in a courtly manner.

Once inside the room, Nic placed Morgan on the bed. She tried to protest, but he placed a finger to her lips in a signal to be silent.

"Morgan, quickly roll over and face the wall," he spoke softly, hearing the footfall of someone coming.

She obeyed just as the door opened. It was the boy from the stables and his three younger sisters carrying heated water from the kitchen. They didn't try to hide their excitement. Few knights came and went in their part of the country, and those who did were not like this one. Most all the knights the boy saw were poor. He couldn't wait to tell his friends.

"Will your squire be all right, my lord?" the boy ventured, growing bold after the third trip of bringing hot water. "He's not going to die is he? I could take his place should you find yourself in need of a new squire. I'm reaching my fifteenth year next month and not yet married, so I don't have a nagging wife to keep me here."

Nic had a hard time keeping a straight face. "Nay, he'll be fine, I think. However, I'll consider your offer for future reference. As to my man there, just a bath and some rest are all he'll need."

The boy cupped his hand over the right side of his mouth and whispered. "Perhaps, my lord, he needs a few riding lessons, too?"

Nic laughed, the warm sound of it resonating through the small room and sliding over Morgan's skin. "You just might be right about those lessons, lad," Nic said, then clasped the teenager on the shoulder.

Morgan, listening to the exchange, didn't take offense. What could she say? He was right. A few riding lessons were in order. Perhaps Nic would train her if she asked him nicely. He wasn't a total brute. In fact, he was far from it. Other than the tirade in the woods, which she fully understood, he was actually very civil.

"I'll be back for the used water in just a while, my lord."

"Here's your coin and thank you for your services. You've done well. Now, off with ya, lad, to tend the animals. We've ridden them hard today," Nic said before he closed the door behind the young man.

When the door was closed tightly, Morgan turned to face her traveling companion. Her eyes slid past Nic to look longingly at the hot bathwater. Nic noticed and didn't blame her. The steaming water was like a siren but her well-being came first.

"Morgan, you must bathe quickly. I'll go get us food. Don't open this door for anyone except me. You understand?"

Morgan answered him with a nod.

"Five minutes, no more, that's all the time you have. I'll be back shortly."

He turned on his heels and left the room.

Morgan bolted the door. Peeling off her sopping clothes and having only five minutes, she didn't bother to wring them out before laying them by the fire to dry.

She sighed as she eased into the tub. The warm water felt heavenly. She couldn't remember the last time she had the luxury of taking a hot bath. Five minutes wasn't enough, but it would have to do; after all, it was five more minutes than she had experienced in the last seven years.

As she quickly bathed, she took in her surroundings. The inn was clean and seemed well run. The room consisted of meager furnishings of a country inn. They served the purpose and Morgan was certainly not going to complain. Compared to her tower room, this was an abundance of luxury.

Placed close to the rare fireplace with an actual working chimney were two chairs and a table at which two could comfortably eat. There was a single stool that had seen better days. The bed, Morgan noticed, was narrow. With Nic's size, it would be a tight fit for him, much less both of them. She was finding the thought of sleeping with him in the close confines of the room discomforting. Toweling off when the knock came, Morgan had mistimed her bath by just a half of a minute.

"Nic?" Morgan softly questioned through the door.

"Aye, lad."

"Give me a minute," she whispered. "I need to cover myself."

Nic sensed her movements in the room, and for a moment, he allowed his imagination to take him to a place that he knew better than to go. He imagined her as she was at the pool: naked, beautiful, and his.

Morgan quickly gathered the bedcover and wrapped herself in it, then unbolted the door and stood behind it to let him enter.

He entered, not sure what he would find when he quickly took stock of the room. Her clothes were neatly spread by the fire to dry. The tub's water was now used. What was even more evident was Morgan wrapped only in a sheet.

Oh my. And that was about all the coherent thought he could muster.

He wasn't some young pup who couldn't control his urges, but she was making it difficult the longer he was around her. He dared not linger, not at the moment, especially knowing she was clean and naked under that wrapping. He needed to allow her to dress without his prying eyes.

"I have found some dry clothes for you, lad." He placed them in the chair and continued. "I'm going back down to see if there's any food I can scrounge. If not, I'll go to the horses for some of our rations. Either way, I'll not be long. Bolt the door behind me."

"Thank you for the bath. I know you didn't have to do that for me." She was very genuine, recognizing that as she was a squire, Nic didn't have to see to that small luxury for her.

His proud smile surprised her as their gaze held each other for a brief second. "Aye, Morgan, I did. And, I did so gladly, but you're welcome all the same."

Chapter 15

Making quick work of binding her breasts and dressing in the clothes Nic had so thoughtfully found, she recognized his steps coming up the stairs.

"It's I, lad." His deep voice eased through the door.

She unbolted then opened the door. He entered carrying a tray of food that smelled delicious. She took the tray and set it down on the table as she deeply breathed in the hearty aroma. As she rearranged the food for them and poured the wine, she heard the rustle of clothing behind her and the soggy flop of them hitting the floor.

Was he undressing? *Of course, you silly girl. He's not letting the opportunity of a warm bath pass by him any more than you would have let it bypass you,* she mentally scolded herself.

She realized that he thought she was a boy so, of course, he would be undressing.

Morgan heard his involuntary sigh escape his lips, and she knew he had silently slipped into the warm water. She wondered as his squire how she could help him with his personal needs. He answered that question almost before the thought was completely formed.

"Morgan, come here and wash my hair, please."

She was behind him, so he couldn't see her face. He heard rather than saw her back into the table.

"Oh, bloody hell," she whispered, then caught the decanter she had nearly knocked over in her retreat.

"Come now, surely you knew you'd have to aid me with my personal needs? And right now, I need you to wash the grime out of my hair. Hurry, the water will cool soon, and I've had enough cold water on me for one day."

His command wasn't abrupt, but Morgan was left in little doubt that she was to follow that order.

Tossing caution to the wind, Morgan placed her hands on his head.

It's just hair, she told herself.

Kneeling at the end of the tub, she gently began to massage his scalp with the coarse cake of soap he had handed her. To counter the way she was feeling, she forced herself to think about the past, not what she was doing.

After the death of her father, the only man she had been this close to was her uncle, and that situation was never pleasant. Until three days ago, when she had taken the spill off the horse, her uncle was the only person to touch her in the last seven years. Morgan tightly closed her eyes against those memories.

She had slept two nights next to this man, had ridden pressed to his body for hours on a horse, and now she was washing his hair while he sat naked in this makeshift tub, which was actually more a deep watering trough. Her initial reaction of uncertainty had given way to curiosity, and she allowed herself to explore further. He was naked in a bathtub, and his sword was across the room. What could he possibly do?

His thick and silky hair rolled through her fingers like the beautifully soft satin ribbons she remembered having as a child. Rubbing his temples and smoothing his brow from the center of his forehead outwards released a flood of memories that she had long buried. Morgan saw her mother doing this to her father while he sat with his eyes closed in his great chair before the fire. Nic was doing much the same.

"My mamma used to do this for my da," she said absently as she moved onto the crown of his head and ran her short nails gently against his scalp. A groan was the byproduct. Gasping, she quickly tried to pull her hands away, but he grabbed her wrists to stop her retreat, heedless of the water he splashed on the floor in the process.

"I'm sorry if I hurt you," she apologized.

"You didn't hurt me, Morgan," he said reassuring her. "That was a moan of contentment. It seems to be soothing my headache."

His grip loosened on her, and he leaned his head back against the rim of the tub. It was far too small for a man of his enormous size. She continued to soap his hair, massaging his scalp. Then, when clean, she rinsed it with water left by the groom for just such a purpose. Nic leaned forward in the small tub, slopping water on the floor and exposing his broad back for Morgan's inspection. She assumed that he wanted her to wash his back, too.

His skin was smooth, tan, and free of any major scars. The few she did see stood out in sharp, white contrast to the tan of the rest of his back. They were scars from many battles, but none threatening, even to her untrained eye.

"You've been lucky, my lord," she commented.

"Thus far, aye, yes, I have." Nic understood what she was saying.

She could see through the murky water a whiter line of skin marking where his breeks hugged and covered his hips, guarding them from the sun. As she continued her ministrations, her body was responding. Her inexperience kept her from realizing the warning signs in him or herself as she continued to touch him out of curiosity as much as necessity.

Nic felt the butterfly touches of her inexperienced hands. He felt the heat coming off her body as she leaned in close to do his bidding. He leaned back in the tub and rested his arms on the narrow rim, then closed his eyes. His legs were so long he had to pull his knees up to fit into the tub. It wasn't enough to hide him from her view.

She was beautiful and he wanted her. It was that simple. He wanted to make love to her more than any other woman he had ever taken to his bed. He purposely allowed her to look at him in his state of full arousal, wanting her to see what she did for him. It would come in handy down the line. She wasn't going to be pleased that he knew she was a duchess and had kept that knowledge from her.

"Oh, now, that's just rude, sir," she gasped and tried to advert her eyes, yet she was curious all the same as she tossed the washcloth over him. It only served to become a tent pole.

Nic softly laughed, "Rude or not, there you have it, a little barrack for all my soldiers."

Morgan shook her head. "You're impossible, sir."

Fully aware of her needs as a woman, he could make love to her in this roadside inn. Her seduction would be child's play.

However, it was too dangerous. So, carnal needs would have to wait. His top priority was getting her to safety and having sex with her would come later. Yet he wasn't made of stone and knew he had to salvage this quickly.

"Never mind me," he said casually with the wave of his hand. "You know how it is sometimes for us men when we fantasize about a beautiful woman. As you can see, the physical effects can be hard to disguise. Now, hurry, lad, and get me a cloth to dry. The bath has grown cold even if I've not." Nic laughed at his pun, knowing he was far from cold for this woman.

She felt quick pangs of jealously rise at the thought of him fantasizing about another woman. Trying to act as unaffected as possible, she quipped before thinking. "Well, sir, might I suggest you do your fantasizing in private. I've no wish to see that thing pointing the way to the northern star," Morgan said.

Nic laughed in delight and relief. "Well put, Morgan. Verray well put."

Morgan had no right to be angry that he was thinking of his woman. Undoubtedly, she would be tiny, blonde, and full breasted; no feminine characteristics Morgan could ever claim to have in her possession. For the first time feelings of inadequacy filtered to the surface, having never really cared before that she had no curves.

She quickly scrambled to her feet to fetch Nic a towel. Rising in one swift movement from the tub, he towered above her with the water sliding off his lethal body.

With towel in hand, she watched in fascination as a single drop made a slow and treacherous journey from his shoulder to his hip. Embarrassed at her own behavior, Morgan avoided his gaze as he took the towel from her just before she turned back to the fire.

Laying his clothes beside hers to dry, Morgan turned her attention to the table as if it were the most interesting item in the world. Nic was behind her. She could feel him, sense him, yet he hadn't touched her. She almost wished he would.

Nic reached out his hand to touch her, but then he smartly pulled back. Thank goodness his better judgment had taken over. Had he touched her, Nic wouldn't have stopped with a kiss and that would have been like opening Pandora's box.

"Where are your clothes?" Morgan asked as Nic made his way to the table and sat down opposite her.

"All clothes in my pack are wet, and I was unable to find a set of dry clothes that fit. I'll just stay as I am until the fire has dried my own."

He had no wish to put the sopping garments back on, not when he had just begun to feel human again. He would dress in the morning and pray he didn't have to fight naked with an enemy. One loose sword was enough.

Nodding and keeping her eyes averted, Morgan had a suspicion that her feelings would show in her face if she looked. Her desire to inspect his unclothed body was strong with curiosity, and it was driving her mad.

She was very quiet again, and Nic could guess the reason. He knew she wanted to look, and perversely, it stroked his male pride.

"Morgan, I know you can speak. You've done so on several occasions. Please, feel free to do so now. I usually don't like having my woman seen and not heard. The same goes for my squire," Nic said, catching his mistake. "You may speak your mind when and how you choose. I'll not insult, beat, or run you through for having an opinion or wishing to carry on conversation with me. It would make for a verray dull or verray deadly existence for both of us."

Before Morgan could answer, a knock came at the door. Nic caught her momentary sharp intake of breath and her look of panic.

"Nic?" she questioned. Her voice was rough from surprise and maybe a little fear.

"It's all right, lad. It's the boy coming back after the water. Quickly hop into bed, turn your back to the door, and cover up as much as possible," he whispered, running his hand down the side of her face in reassurance before turning her to the bed. If she noticed the gesture as odd for a man touching a boy, she kept it to herself. More than likely, it didn't register through the spike of adrenaline running through her system, resulting from the fear of being discovered with him unarmed and nearly naked.

He remedied the unarmed part by picking up his sword before answering the door. Nic knew it paid to be careful.

Morgan giggled at the sight of her knight's only armor being an old bedsheet.

She quickly did as she was told just as Nic opened the door to allow the boy and two others to come remove the dirty water.

"He's better, my lord?" the boy asked keeping his voice lowered as the girls left with pails in both hands.

"Aye, he is," Nic said then smiled with good nature. "A warm bath and dry clothes are doing wonders for his disposition. He's sleeping more naturally. All in all we were lucky. I think he'll be fine to get on the road come morning."

"What are ye instructions for me, sir," the boy asked respectfully.

"We shall break our fast at four and take our leave before the sun is up."

"As ye wish, sir. I'll have the horses ready for ye."

"Good. Do just that and I'll have another coin for you. Now, be a good lad and run along."

The boy eased out the door, taking the remainder of the dirty water with him along with a story to tell his grandchildren.

Nic closed the door softly behind him. Throwing the bolt, he turned back to Morgan just as she rolled over.

Nic guarded his expression.

It's just as well that Morgan can't read my mind, he thought.

His thoughts were far from pure. After all, he never claimed to be a monk. Seeing her there on the bed looking clean, warm, and inviting was killing him. The firelight was playing off the crown of her hair, the warm flickers turning her smooth skin to a translucent glow. Wisely, he kept his thoughts and his hands to himself.

"Come, Morgan. Let us eat while we have the opportunity to eat something warm."

He didn't have to ask twice as she jumped from the bed, letting the quilt fall to the floor behind her. She was starving. Quickly going to the side facing the fire, she sat at the well-worn but serviceable table.

"My lord, you need to sit closer to the fire to keep from getting cold. You're without a shirt." A fact she was painfully aware of, and one she really didn't have to remind him of either.

"Your thoughtfulness is appreciated, Morgan."

Nic didn't argue. He would have sat there anyway. If he were to sit where she was sitting, it would place his back to the door, which was something he wasn't likely to do any time soon.

107

Nic served their platters. She looked longingly at the food as he placed it in front of her. Nic thought she looked like a well-trained animal, patiently waiting until he had taken the first bite to begin eating with relish. It made him almost angry. Only heavy-handed dominance fostered this behavior.

"Oh, this is wonderful!" Morgan closed her eyes and moaned in delight as she took the first bites of the meal. Her eyes were alive as she spoke. "It has been years since I had anything warm to eat. I'd almost forgotten how good it could be to have the warmth slide down my throat."

Coming from any other woman, Nic would have looked for sexual innuendo in the words. However, he watched her in fascination at her childlike enjoyment of the simple act of eating a warm meal. Furthermore, her statement confused him. They had been on the road only three days, and surely she hadn't been on the run for more than a day or so before he found her. So what did she mean? Could her being the duchess be a mistake?

"Morgan, what do you mean you haven't had a warm meal in years?" Nic hadn't intended the words to come out as a command for an answer. He studied her and her reaction wasn't what Nic had expected.

She quickly lowered her head, closed her eyes, and placed her hands into her lap. It was as if she was bracing herself for the blow she was so sure would follow.

He watched her for a moment more, eyes narrowing, trying to read her body language.

Was she cowering? Or was she just watchful?

"Please, I beg your forgiveness," she said. The tears slide down her cheeks. The last few days were getting to her. She knew Nic wouldn't strike her, yet old habits die hard.

Nic saw that all joy was gone from her as she fell back into the silence that Nic was growing to hate.

"I'm not angry with you, Morgan. Eat your food while it's still warm," he encouraged her gently.

Morgan didn't eat another bite nor did she say another word as Nic continued with his meal. She wouldn't meet his gaze, keeping her head lowered and eyes averted. The tension was thick between them, and he was angry with an enemy he didn't know but was growing in his suspicions.

To break the tension, Nic began to tell her stories of court, of London, and the king.

It did the trick.

As he shared his experiences, she reappeared, inching past her caution. Her curiosity was stronger than the lingering wariness that she surely still felt towards him.

She sat in awe of the stories and began slowing eating again, so he continued to fill her mind with information that he felt she might find useful in the future while she filled her belly.

Her mind absorbed every detail, every word. He saw she couldn't get enough, like a sponge taking in everything her hungry mind could absorb. Making a note to add that to the list of traits he was discovering about her, he could tell by looking into her eyes that there was a great intelligence there. He would feed that intelligence with each new adventure he passed on to her, especially if it distracted her enough to feed her physical body, as well.

With one last tale, he went on to talk about the swordplay that occurred between knights, explaining it as a way to keep his stamina up, his blade quick, and just to let off steam and energy. He talked about different offensive and defensive moves. He told her how to defend herself from an attacker. He talked of where the killing points were on a body using the uneaten bird as a model.

"Will you teach me? Please?" She ventured the question, biting her bottom lip and praying she hadn't overstepped her boundaries with this knight.

The question surprised him, tempting him to quickly say aye.

"We'll see." He smiled patiently. That was all he would commit to in that moment.

Her face was an open book for him to read. It amazed him the way her eyes sparkled in the firelight as he talked and then how her disappointment was clear when he stopped and began to ready for bed.

She was so wrapped up in his stories she had forgotten all about his state of undress. Her eyes were having trouble staying focused on his face.

He's beautiful, she thought.

And, to her mortification, he was speaking to her and she had been staring. She snapped her gaze back to his face.

Nic smiled secretively to himself. He knew her body and inexperience were wreaking havoc with her senses. Hell, even he was having a hard time keeping his hands off her. The draw between them was unmistakable and would become more so as time passed. However, she was inexperienced, and he wouldn't take advantage of her until he properly married her before Henry and the priest. It was up to him to keep the lines clearly drawn.

"You may sleep by the fire or in the bed. It's your choice, lad."

He knew he was sleeping in the bed either way. He wasn't about to pass up a mattress for a stone floor. He made the offer instinctively, knowing Morgan had to feel the choice was hers to make. Nic saw the indecision on her face but knew the soft mattress would prove too much temptation for her to decline. She walked to the bed and lay down. He walked across the room to join her, his towering form standing by the edge of the narrow frame.

"Morgan, roll over. I need to be between you and the door so that I can protect you from intruders if necessary."

She almost panicked, knowing that would trap her between the wall and the wall of Nic's body.

Nay, she thought, *I'll be strong.* She would play the part of his squire.

"Nay, I'll protect you, my lord." And she felt she might actually do that very thing and die trying. He was a good man who reminded her of her father, not in looks but in manner. That was what counted. "It would gain you extra time to draw your sword should an intruder enter. They would have to come past me first," she said as she stood to face him.

Nic might have found this humorous if he had given the comment any thought or if they had been in any other circumstance. However, since he didn't stop to think and they were not in a different place, his reaction proved swift.

"Nay," he said emphatically.

She wondered how one uncomplicated word could carry such weight.

"I repeat, nay." Nic crossed his arms over his chest. "You don't have a weapon, nor do I know if you could use it even if you did own one. Now, get in bed and let me do what I do best, or go sleep by the fire."

He knew he had challenged her but figured the soft bed would likely win in the end, and she would do as he asked by sleeping on the inside.

She looked into his handsome face for a few seconds and saw all she needed to see. Morgan had not lived this long without learning the lesson of when to pick her battles. This one was one she wasn't likely to win. It wasn't worth the energy to wage the battle, either. Furthermore, he wasn't going to force her into compliance and have her back to a wall.

Fine, she thought, *I'll sleep by the fire.*

Morgan's blanket was in her pack by the plank door to their room. Without a word, she began to make her way toward the door.

Mistaking her intent, Nic was on Morgan before she knew what was happening. Whirling her around, his hands an iron grip on her upper arms, Nic pinned the full length of her body to the door with his.

"Don't be foolish, lad" he demanded.

"Let me go," she whispered.

He didn't hear her words.

"There's at least one search party out there looking for ya, lad, and who knows how many more. Did you think I wasn't aware the hunters are after you like some prize game? You're mine, and I don't intend to let harm find you. So do not be rash and think to walk out of here, Morgan. You would be making a most grave mistake were you to try and leave."

Nic felt her tighten against his body. Her resolve began to rise within her.

With determination, she met him squarely. Her eyes narrowed and her chin rose. Slowly she shook her head. "Nay, Nic. The mistake is already yours to own. My intent wasn't to walk out the door but to get my blanket from my pack and sleep by the fire."

Nic looked down to where she was pointing on the floor by her feet.

Coolly, she continued to deliver her warning. "You will release me and don't touch me again, sir. I may be your squire, but I'm your squire by choice and by agreement. I need something from you. You need something from me. It's just that simple. Furthermore, I'll walk out any door I choose and at any time of my choosing. Don't ever forget that, McKinnon."

Holding his hands up in concession, Nic let her go and backed away a step. He was angry with himself as the silence hung thick between them and as he stood watching her pick up her pack. Morgan pushed past him, walking to the fire without a backward glance, and Nic knew any forward progress he may have made with his bride had just been undone.

~*****~

The inn was quiet, and still Nic couldn't sleep. He kept seeing the caged animal peering out of those beautiful green eyes. He had somehow found a raw, open wound in her when he backed her to a wall. She came out fighting. Whatever Morgan was running from may have put mistrust and fear into her, but it had not broken her spirit.

He smiled. He found the thought pleasing.

It would be a shame to break such a creature. Her mistrust was deep but her spirit was stronger, and his respect for her deepened as he thought about the fact that she had planned and carried out her escape. Granted, it had been far from perfect, but the fact she had tried and succeeded was commendable.

On the other hand, was it just a last act of desperation?

Was the unknown less frightening than the life she left behind?

Where was she heading when he found her? Nic hadn't thought about that aspect. Had Morgan prepared to stay on her own? She had no way of knowing she would find her way to be here with him as her protector. So even as appalling as the thought might be, Nic felt certain that was exactly what she was planning.

The questions swirled through his head as he pushed unwanted images from his mind of the horrors that could have happened had he not found her when he did. She may not be aware of the evils of this world, but he was no stranger to the viler side of life.

He kept looking over at her sleeping on her side by the fire, noting the soft curves of her body outlined by the glow of the dying embers. The fire would be dead soon and she would get cold, but it would serve her right. She could have had the warmth and softness of the bed but made the choice to sleep on the floor instead. It was her choice.

Nevertheless, Nic knew it really wasn't her choice. He had forced her to the fire just as he had tried to force her to the inside wall.

"Well, fine. You win, lass," he said as he padded over to her, knelt down, and gathered her as if she were a sleeping child. Gently, Nic laid her on the bed. She never stirred as he pulled her to him.

She's a heavy sleeper and I'm grateful, he thought.

The last thing he wanted in the wee hours before dawn was another argument with her.

"Stubborn wench. Little do you realize that you do belong to me," he whispered into the night as he pulled her closer into his warmth.

Chapter 16

"My lord, the mounts are ready to ride." The young boy whispered to Nic as he stood in the darkened hallway.

Outside it was very predawn and hours before morning prayers. It was time to leave. Nic had gone to ready the horses for travel, leaving Morgan sleeping in the narrow bed upstairs. They had to keep moving because to delay was inconceivable with the search party probably just hours behind them.

The young man, true to his word, had the mounts ready to go before first light. Nic went back into the inn to retrieve his bride. In the room, he lifted her into his arms carefully, taking the chance of waking her. Morgan barely stirred.

"Go back to sleep, Morgan," he said gently, pushing her head into the curve of his shoulder.

Making his way through the common room with her in his arms, he edged past sleeping travelers, never noticing the man in the shadows.

"Ah, yes," Stewart said under his breath.

The McKinnon was carrying the girl, who was wrapped in his cloak. Yet he could see her face as her head rested on Nic's shoulder. Stewart was positive he had found his prey. She was with the knight that the drunken thief told him about while complaining about his loses in the Bristol pub.

Stewart slipped unnoticed out the side door.

~*****~

Morgan woke slowly to a gentle rocking movement. The faint light told her it was early dawn. Safe and warm, she

115

didn't want to come out of her sleep-filled paradise. There she was loved, cherished, and protected.

She inhaled deeply, then slowly let out the air in her lungs as she breathed a sigh of relief. She knew where she was. She was on a horse and in Nic's arms. To her surprise it felt safe, regardless of the misunderstanding they had the night before. She felt something she had not felt in years: protected and totally secure.

Nic knew the minute Morgan woke. Her body went from soft and malleable to alert. He felt her stiffen shortly after leaving the inn. Nic braced himself for what he felt sure was coming. Then to his surprise, she relaxed against him again; he had never expected her to go back to sleep.

He enjoyed holding her. It made him feel good to know he could give her a few moments of peace and security. She had finally given him her trust in that respect, maybe not in him as a man, but she did have faith in him to protect her, and he would defend her to his death. Honor had nothing to do with it, he realized. She was worth dying for.

She was stirring, coming alive again. Looking into her face in the early gray light of dawn, her gaze was unfocused and looked as if she were far away, in a distant place.

"You smell the way my father smelled, like rich earth, hot flames, and crashing seas. I miss him," she said with the sorrow clear in her voice.

It caught him off guard.

"Morgan," he breathed her name and leaned in to kiss her. Abruptly stopping, he realized what he was doing.

Changing like quicksilver, she straightened, stiffening in his arms as she gained control.

"Nic, I really do understand the need to have me play the role of your injured squire while we were at the inn. That's no longer necessary. You can put me down now. I can ride on my own. It's safer that way."

Would he ever figure this woman out? Shaking his head, he stopped Trojan and allowed her to slide down his leg to the ground, all the while holding her arms to prevent her from tumbling. Walking back to her mount, Nic watched as her hips gently swayed in the boy's trousers that she had donned in the night.

He made a mental note to find her some looser clothing. That sweet little bottom and long legs were proving to be a distraction that he didn't need and certainly didn't want.

She eased alongside him as Trojan danced sideways. "Set whatever pace you feel necessary to get us safely to London. I'll do my best to keep up."

Following her suggestion, Nic set a moderately brisk pace, though not as grueling as the previous day. In the clear light of the day, Morgan decided she was acting immature for being jealous. She clearly had no reason. Nor did she have a right. He wasn't her knight. He was, although, her employer in a manner of speaking, and she owed him respect.

For years after her parents' death, she had prayed for a knight to rescue her. Seemingly, on the surface fate answered her prayer. However, there was no way she could let her girlhood fantasies run away with her. She was a grown woman and understood how fantasy and reality rarely crossed paths, and she knew that better than most.

She was no longer a child and had to look at the bigger picture. And that bigger picture was getting to London and talking to the king. When they arrived in London, Morgan wasn't beyond using Nic's connections to get through the outer gates of the palace. She wouldn't need him once she spoke to the king and made her identity known. At least, Morgan hoped she wouldn't need him. Still, she contemplated that she wouldn't burn that bridge until she was fully certain. He was a man she didn't mind having as her ally.

Besides, it was obvious his affections lay elsewhere. His body the night before in the bath was evidence of that fact. His very open and honest confession only confirmed it. And she wasn't totally ignorant of how sex worked. He had been aroused. So was she, and those were waters she didn't need to explore.

Images of him kissing the blonde, faceless woman came uninvited into her mind. She imagined Nic with those large and beautifully tanned hands framing the face of his woman. She could see Nic slowly lower his mouth to his lover's lips, his hair cascading to cloak both his and his lover's faces. She shook herself out of the vision, feeling the jealousy arise anew and much more fiercely than before.

What is wrong with me, she wondered.

She attempted to harden her heart.

Once they arrived in London, she would tell him of her true identity. He would be bound by rules of court to escort her to the king. Simply put, she outranked him in polite society.

Morgan felt she must get free of Nic as soon as he had helped her secure that introduction with King Henry.

He's as dangerous to my person as Uncle Lester ever thought to be, even at his worst, she thought.

It was a different kind of danger, but danger, nonetheless. He was a danger to her heart.

Why was Nic not toothless and old? At least then she could feel more detached.

Lost in his own thoughts, Nic hardly noticed the landscape changing as they made their way eastward on a well-traversed road. His thoughts were just as dark as Morgan's. Lord Brentwood must be to blame for her apprehensive behavior; there could be no other explanation for her leaving Seabridge in the first place and her fear of going back.

Nic also recognized that she didn't fear him any longer. It was more that she distrusted him. Morgan obviously led him away from Seabridge because she had sufficient reason to run. Not striking him as a woman to run simply as a way to gain attention, he was sure Morgan made her escape for a very good reason. Her behavior only sealed his conclusions. And after the last night's events, how was he going to persuade her to confide in him? He knew he had severely damaged his chances with her. It was obvious the lady didn't trust easily, and he needed her to trust him. He needed to be able to size up his enemy, and the only way to do that was to get the information from her.

He slowed the pace. Leaning over, he grabbed Salt's bridle, stopping them on the road. He saw the look she gave him. She was wary and rightfully so after his behavior the night before.

"Forgive me for last night. I was wrong." He offered up an olive branch. "I overreacted just as I overreacted in the woods. I can be a grouch when sleep deprived, and I have never tried to claim sainthood because of it."

"Probably just as well, my lord," she offered. She wasn't letting him so easily off the hook even if she understood.

He doesn't want me to run, Morgan thought as she looked down at his hands holding the reins.

Turning to face him, she could see the set of his jaw as he looked at a spot between Trojan's ears. He was collecting his thoughts. She could almost hear the wheels turning.

He faced her squarely. "Morgan, again, I'm verray sorry about last night and would ask your forgiveness for my behavior. It was uncalled for. I know that you don't trust easily, and I've my suspicions as to why. So, I know that what I'm about to ask isn't going to be easy for you."

"What is it you want, Nic?"

"I'm asking you to take a leap of faith and place your trust in me even if I have yet to earn it."

Nic waited. She said nothing, committed to nothing.

He had more to say. "You must tell me why you're so afraid of Brentwood and why you're running from Seabridge. If you want me to protect you, then I have to know what kind of battlements I'm up against."

He had been wise in grabbing the reins of her horse. Nic saw the sudden emotions flash across her face. What he saw wasn't necessarily fear, but it certainly was suspicion. As transparent as she was to him, he knew her first reaction was to run. He knew it right away.

"Nay, Morgan, trying to run again is too dangerous. I'm not the enemy and what's more, when you search your heart, you know it."

He waited for her acknowledgment which came in the form of the simple nod of her head. "You're under my protection and can trust me. You're as safe with me as if in your father's arms. Even if I don't own you, as you've so eloquently reminded me last night, I've sworn to protect you, lad, something I'll do to my death if need be."

"Where is this going?" Morgan asked.

"I must know who and what I face, or I'll face that enemy blind."

Morgan studied her companion's face. All she saw when she looked into his eyes was the truth. Should she tell him? She wanted to.

How had they gone from strangers to her wanting to confide in him in so short a time? She still knew nothing about him. Yet she really did know all she needed to know. He was decent and honorable. She wanted to share her concerns with him, but the minute she did she would lose the advantage. She would no longer be able to masquerade as a squire, and even if he might not know she was the Duchess of Seabridge, he would know she wasn't a boy. It would change everything.

On the other hand, if she withheld the information, then he would blindly walk into a confrontation with her uncle.

Nic saw the inner struggle. He knew what she felt was her dilemma. If she told him, her cover was blown. He didn't dare tip his hand and let her know he already knew she was a woman. He didn't want a confrontation arising from her realizing he had known. She would think that he had played her for a fool, which was far from the truth.

He was learning not to corner her, but pressure her he would.

"You must tell me, Morgan. If I'm to protect you, I must have the truth."

Morgan wasn't ready to give in as she looked away.

Nic shook his head and sighed. It was just as he thought. Morgan told him nothing and everything with her look, but it wasn't enough. He needed to know, and he would have the truth before it was all done and over with.

It would have to wait. Fate stepped back in.

"Bloody hell!" Nic suddenly cursed. He tensed and in a flash, put his spurs to Trojan. "Hang on!"

Like she really had any other choice.

Chapter 17

Still gripping Morgan's horse's reins, Nic pulled her along, leaving her to hold on for dear life. Then she figured out why he was in such a hurry just as an arrow whizzed by her head. The second one passed through flesh. She screamed from the searing pain that followed.

Nic, unaware one of the arrows had connected with tender flesh, was making a line for the woods to find what cover he could.

He pulled her unceremoniously from Salt's back. "Quickly! Hide in that underbrush. Don't, and I repeat, don't come out no matter what you think you see or hear! Stay hidden, but if they capture you, lad, fight with everything you've got! Don't go quietly! Now, go!"

Dumbfounded, Morgan found herself pushed under the brush as Nic wheeled around, and with a great war cry, began to engage the assailants. She couldn't see anything past the underbrush. Nevertheless, she certainly was beginning to grasp what was going on around her as she heard one man fall, and then another.

She didn't know how many were attacking them, but Nic had just killed another man, making three dead for sure. The man fell close enough for her to see the dirt under his nails of the hand Nic had severed before dealing the deathblow. That hand was still clutching a dagger. Without thinking, she reached out and pried the dagger from the dead man's fingers. In doing so, she edged out far enough to see the extent of the battle raging around her.

Oh, God, he needs help! Her only thought was for him.

Morgan felt his skill was more than average, and he was exceptionally good with a sword. *But nobody could stand against three more men alone*, she thought.

Without thinking, Morgan scrambled out from under the brush, rushing the closest man. With one fluid

123

movement, she plunged the dagger into one of the killing points that Nic had shown her just the night before. The man fell, clutching his throat, gasping for the breath that would never come.

Without breaking stride, she scooped up the dying man's sword and rushed the next man. Catching him off guard, she briefly had the advantage. Coming in low and fast, Morgan pushed her shoulder into the tackle, putting the man on his back. Unfortunately, she fell on top of him. In one swift countermovement, he rolled her onto her back. She dropped the sword in the process.

Straddling her, he pressed her fully into the soft forest floor, bearing his full weight on her abdomen. She couldn't breathe from the crushing weight, and his fingers wrapped tightly around her throat. She knew that she could never win this fight. The man had the advantage of strength and size. This adversary would kill her if she didn't stay alive long enough to give Nic time to kill the man, but he was engaged in his own deathly fight.

Their entanglement was a fierce and a swiftly moving battle. Both men knew only one would walk away. She prayed it would be Nic, but she remembered that God helps those who help themselves.

Morgan had narrowed her vision. Her focus trained to tuning out everything excluding the man on top of her. Nic was on his own.

"Fight with everything you've got," Nic had said.

She was doing just that. Her attacker had just sliced her face, and she managed a lucky shot to the man's right eye, snapping his head and upper body back, giving her a clear shot to his chest. By some twist of fate, he dropped the dagger. She quickly picked it up.

Fight with everything you've got…. Nic's words echoed in her head. *Don't go quietly.*

She plunged the dagger in as deeply as she could but it wasn't enough to kill him. She twisted the knife as he grabbed her around the throat again. He began to squeeze in earnest, slowly choking the life from her body, crushing her airway. Morgan gasped for breath; black circles hovered in front of her eyes.

She knew she was dying. Her airway was collapsing.

Fight, damn it, fight, her brain screamed to her oxygen-deprived muscles. The burning in her lungs was increasing as if she had inhaled hot coals. Reaching up, she found the strength to pull the dagger out of his chest and sliced his wrist. The slice was just enough for him to release his death grip around her throat. He batted the knife from her hand. She drew in a great gulp of air as her hands were instinctively flailing around for anything she could use for a weapon.

As if guided by a higher power, her hand touched something cold and rough.

Her assailant hit her again, and then, from somewhere deep within her, she began to feel her power rise. Her will to live was strong. Stronger than she even thought possible. She wanted to live! She wanted to live! Live to see the sunset. Live to have children. Live to grow old.

"Now, Morgan!" Her mother's voice filled her with courage and strength as she grabbed the stone. Either he would die or she would, and it wasn't going to be her! She had to make that one shot count or he would surely deliver the killing blow. With all the strength remaining in her, she swung hard. Morgan felt the hard stone connect with softer bone and heard the breaking of the man's skull.

The momentum of the blow forced him off of her, relieving the crush to her chest. The man rolled one more time, and Morgan plunged the dagger into his throat, making sure he would never rise again. He would hurt her no more.

Morgan painstakingly got to her knees just in time to see Nic strike the deadly blow to his opponent, whose head was severed from his neck.

On the forest floor, with blood running down her face and shoulder, she wondered why she was losing so much blood. Then she realized that the arrow must have struck an artery, a fatal wound if not treated quickly.

With the danger of the attack past, Morgan knew she was in trouble. Looking up at Nic, who stood frozen in his last move of attack, their gazes locked in the deadly quiet of the forest. All she heard was Nic's ragged and labored breathing and the pounding of her heart in her ears. Morgan's vision was narrowing. The sight of Nic was fading fast.

"Help me."

Her tiny voice broke through his fog.

With all strength gone, Morgan was no longer able hold herself up and shook uncontrollably as she collapsed to the forest floor. Nic saw she was losing blood at an alarming rate. Too soon she would go into shock.

"Don't dare die on me, Morgan," he commanded as he went into action.

"Another command I may not be able to follow," she said before falling unconscious.

Nic was in agony as he quickly did a field dressing to stem the bleeding. How many times had he dressed a wound for one of his fallen men? A hundred? A thousand? It had never been more important than this minute for him to do it right.

Scooping her unconscious body off the forest floor, he whistled for Trojan. It was miraculous that Salt and Vernon hadn't fled. Trojan would have had no choice except to follow with their bridles still attached to his. Nic carried Morgan to his mount. It wasn't the most gentle of movements, and he thanked God that she was unconscious as he flung her over his horse's neck and mounted behind her. Then he gently turned her and cradled her in his arms. She was bleeding, but not as freely. That was lucky, and he would take what luck he could find.

He had to get her to safety, but where? London was too far and going back to the inn would surely deliver her back into the arms of her uncle.

Featherstone Castle, he thought.

Nic pushed the horses unmercifully. There was no choice. Morgan's life was at stake.

Chapter 18

"Open the gates!" The shout of the sentry echoed through the bailey. "It's Sir Nic. Hurry, man, and open the gates!"

The guardsman turned to his son who had come running at the sound of the commotion. "Quick, lad, run. Go get Connor."

Nic rode Trojan full tilt into the courtyard of the home of his friend Lord Connor Holden, Earl of Featherstone. He came to an abrupt halt just feet from the main doorway as Connor stepped through it with sword in hand, ready for battle.

When he saw his close friend, Connor ran to Nic, then reached up to take Morgan as Nic handed his precious bundle to him. Connor took her into his arms, allowing Nic to dismount. Nic quickly took her back into his arms, wanting to carry Morgan into the castle. She was his burden and he would bear it gladly.

Connor was more than just a little surprised and shocked to see Nic with a bloody, unconscious boy in his arms.

"Nic, what in God's holy name happened? You look as if you've the devil on your heels and had a fight or two with him along the way. Come, inside. What can I do?" Connor quickly led his friend and the bundle he carried into the castle and behind the walls to safety.

Nic bellowed his command to the servants. Without a backward glance, he took the stone steps two at a time. He didn't wait to see if the housekeeper carried out his orders. "I need warmed blankets, boiling water, clean bandages, a bath, a fine needle, and silk thread brought to my chamber!"

He had no doubt they would obey his orders. He was a long-standing friend and frequent visitor. He made his way to his usual chamber with Connor just steps behind.

With gentleness one would never think a man as large as Nic could muster, he placed Morgan on top of the coverlets, oblivious to the fact that he wasn't alone in the room.

He began to rub her arms to get the warmth back into them, being careful of her wounds. Quietly, soothingly, he began to speak.

"Come on, Morgan. Come back to me. Morgan?" He paused. "Morgan?" He waited in vain for a response he feared wasn't to come. "Come on. Please, come back to me."

Nothing came from her. She didn't stir. The bright red blood covering her body stood out in stark contrast to the crisp white of the cool linen sheets. She was still as death.

So much blood, Nic thought. *Too much blood.*

"You're a fighter! Fight, damn it! Fight! Where are the blankets and water?" Nic shouted.

Connor found this scene remarkable. He had known Nic for the better part of his life, and he had never before seen the man anything except cool and collected. He was the one usually losing his patience. Connor had never seen Nic this emotional and surely never emotional over a squire. Something about this scene didn't fit.

Connor put words to his misgivings.

"Nic, you left me a week ago. Now, you show back up on my doorstep with a boy who you have grown attached to quickly. Care to tell me what exactly is going on here?"

Nic turned to face his friend who was leaning against the doorframe of the room, his massive bulk nearly filling the door opening. Except for his younger brother Cullen, Connor was the only man Nic knew who could match his size and build.

"Nay now, Connor. I must get Morgan revived first. Her safety is paramount."

"Her?" Connor looked at his friend, his dark head tilted to the right, his left eyebrow raised in surprise. "Hmmm, well that explains at least one thing."

Connor pushed away from the doorframe to make way for the servants. The kitchen boys were bringing in the tub, along with the food and extra blankets that Nic had demanded.

Connor was beginning to see just how dirty and bloody Nic was, too.

"Nic, my friend, let Mary take care of Morgan while you tend to your own needs. It would be best."

"Nay, if Morgan wakes up, it'll be to unfamiliar surroundings. I need to be here to ensure there's no fight. I don't want the bleeding to start again. That's something we can't afford."

Connor was looking at his longtime friend with an expression of puzzlement.

Nic continued. He didn't want Connor pressuring him for answers, and certainly not with an audience looking on. Saying that Connor was an impatient man was a huge understatement, like saying the sun was only mildly necessary for life.

"It's a story even I don't have all the pieces to just yet, my friend. Nevertheless, trust me in this, Connor. Morgan needs me to be here."

Connor was beginning to think Nic needed to be here, too, even if the man wasn't aware of his reasons. Connor also noted Nic didn't refer to Morgan as she in front of the house staff. He would respect Nic's obvious wish for this piece of information to remain a secret. At least for the moment, it would remain between the two of them.

"Is any of that blood on you yours?" Connor knew it would be like his friend to neglect his own needs and place his total focus on the woman.

Nic looked at Morgan's swollen and purple face, then examined the arrow wound on her upper shoulder. He was thankful that the bleeding had stopped. His dressing had preserved her life, and if infection didn't set in, it might have saved her arm, too.

"None to speak of, nay, just minor cuts. Morgan took the worst of it. I could use some fresh clothes."

"You know what is mine is yours, my friend, you've but to ask what you need. I'll have Keegan bring them to you. When you feel you can leave your squire for a time, I'll be in my solar."

With a nod from Nic, Connor left the room in search of his valet.

In the meantime, while waiting for fresh clothes, Nic tended Morgan's wounds as best as he could and prayed. After bolting the chamber door, he stripped his bloody clothes off, then his bride's. Gathering her in his arms, he padded over to the extra-large bronze tub filled with bucket after bucket of clean, hot water. She still felt cold against his naked flesh. Needing to raise her body temperature, Nic gently lowered himself into the hot water, cradling her and tenderly washing her as a mother would a young child. Her bloody clothes gone, Morgan looked fragile, especially with her wounds.

Her narrow waist was showing signs of bruising, especially around her rib cage where she had taken the full weight of the man straddling her. He ran his hands down each side, probing for cracked or broken bones. Satisfied she suffered none, Nic moved his attentions to her face. Her beautiful features were purple, her eyes swollen shut from the blows. The knife wound from her hairline to her jaw was deep and jagged. The tiny stitches he used to bring the seam together would help to lessen the scar, but she would bear it always.

For her it would be a constant reminder of this horrific day.

For him it would be an invariable testament of how close he came to losing her, punctuating his failure to protect her.

"I'm verray sorry, Morgan. I should never've let this happen to you." He apologized, gently brushing his lips to her forehead.

Her soft lips were bloody and swollen from the blows her attacker had inflicted on her. The finger marks were visible along the column of her graceful neck, showing ugly and purple against white tender flesh.

Her shoulder was a mess. The arrow had taken a chunk of her upper arm, severing the artery as it passed through. There was nothing to do for it except keep it clean.

All this was damning evidence against him of just how close he had come to losing her. When she improved, he would choke her himself for her impulsive actions, even though her response had been brave. This was twice she had disobeyed him. Both times, it nearly cost her life.

He remembered her final words before falling unconscious, "Another command I may not be able to follow." A tiny smile of irony grabbed his lips.

However, he was grateful for those actions. He probably could have taken them all on and killed them. They weren't highly trained, but a ragtag group of highwaymen. Yet he felt sure it wouldn't have happened without a great degree of harm to him personally. It was by her actions alone that he walked away from the encounter with just a couple of minor wounds.

Nic placed Morgan, clean from the bath and no longer covered in blood, under the covers of the massive bed where he had slept as more than just a guest. Featherstone was like home to him. He had known Connor most all his life. Now Nic felt he was in Connor's debt for more than just his friendship.

Nic dressed slowly, as if he had aged over the course of the last few hours. He felt drained and lost for the first time in his life.

After he ate from the tray of food Mary had brought him, he sat, watching Morgan as she lay there. Her breathing seemed labored and unsteady. He knew Mary was praying in the chapel and he thought he should join her. Instead, he stayed by Morgan's bed, having asked Mary to intercede on his behalf.

Needing to feel her in his arms, he gave in to the urge to go to her, to hold her. Nic crawled onto the bed, pulling her against his body, immediately feeling better. It felt right. This was where she belonged.

Was Morgan his destiny? He thought perhaps she just might be. Connor was right. Fate was a crafty witch and Destiny even more cruel. He had just found Morgan and might lose her.

Hours went by. He released her only to light the candles by the bedside.

As the candles burned low, Nic began to realize her breathing was back to normal. Her body temperature had risen. She was in a natural slumber. Only then did he, too, succumb to sleep.

~*****~

Morgan stirred as she sensed Nic's presence next to her. She could barely see the single candle burning low through the tiny slits of her swollen eyelids. Where was she? The last memory she had was of the fight.

"Nic, are you hurt?" Morgan spoke softly, reaching out to touch him. Her mouth and throat were so dry, and it was painful to speak.

"I'm unharmed. It's all right. Don't panic and don't try to talk. Drink this, just small sips," he said, bringing a cup of warm liquid to her lips.

"Thank you," she said after taking a few sips of the warm broth. "Where are we?"

Brushing the hair back from her forehead, he checked her for fever. It was slight and not unexpected. "We're in the house of friends who welcomed us. You're safe, and so's your secret. Morgan, I know you're the Duchess of Seabridge."

He waited a moment to let his news register with her.

Morgan found that she was relieved that the secret was out and in the open.

"If you send me back, he'll kill me." Morgan tried to stay strong. "Are you going to send me back?"

Nic shook his head. Not on his life would he send her back. "Nay, Morgan. I won't send you back," Nic said.

Finally losing the battle with her emotions, she began to sob, relieved yet frightened of what her future would bring.

"Please, don't weep. I promise I'll keep you safe." In order to soothe her, Nic placed her in his lap and wrapped a sheet around her shoulders.

She continued to sob. "Thank you, thank you." She felt safe for the first time in seven years. The relief was overwhelming. "I'm sorry you got dragged into this situation. I fear that Uncle Lester will kill you for this."

"Nay, he won't. Please, Morgan, love, listen to me. Please, stop. You're safe. I'm safe." Nic could feel her sobbing still and wanted to soothe her. "Morgan, it'll be fine. I promise. I know that I've let you down before. Never again, I promise."

He felt her nod her head against his chest, sniffing loudly. She still believed in him even though he had let her down. He almost had gotten her killed.

Morgan quieted and tiny hiccups escaped her as he continued to hold her and ran his hand rhythmically up and down her arm without saying anything. He felt her relaxing against him.

"Morgan, love, are you better?"

She nodded her head, confessing, "It has just all been too much." Seven years of too much, she wanted to say but held back. "I guess I just needed to let it out."

"Hmmm," he grunted, not fully understanding. Nic guessed letting it out by crying was something a woman needed to do. If he needed to *let it out* he would just have a grueling practice session with Connor or Cullen. He wondered if he would ever understand the fairer sex. Maybe he didn't have to understand her to make her happy? Perhaps acceptance of her was all that was required.

"I need to go downstairs and talk to Connor. I haven't left your side. Now that you know we're safe and you're not in any danger, do you think you'll be all right by yourself for little while? I'll stay if you wish it."

She shook her head. "Nay, take your leave and go to your friend."

"I promise to come back and check on you later. Try to sleep more, lass. You need to rest to regain your strength. Do you want me to blow out the candle or leave it burning?"

"Burning, please. I'm afraid of the dark." Morgan's graveled voice was barely above a whisper.

Nic rested his chin on her head and stared at the far wall. Anger grew within him as he could only guess what Brentwood had done to her.

"I'll make Brentwood pay," Nic vowed hotly.

When she stiffened, he drew his anger deep within himself.

"My anger is at your uncle, never at you, Morgan, never you," he reassured her, continuing to rub her back in slow circular motions.

He waited for her to relax again.

"Get some sleep, lass. I'll return shortly," he said, then placed her gently on the bed. Next, he tucked the blankets around her and left the chamber, which he had not left for the past two days.

Chapter 19

Nic found Connor in the Great Hall by the fire. He
motioned for Nic to take the chair beside him.

"What in the bloody hell have you gotten yourself into
this time?" Connor demanded, handing Nic a mug of spiced
wine.

"That battered and bloody young squire of mine is
actually Morgan Pembridge."

"Your duchess?" Connor asked with more than mild
interest.

"Aye."

Connor whistled through his teeth.

"All right, so she is your bride. Can you tell me what's
going on? How did this all come about? If she's the
duchess then why is she dressed as a boy? More
importantly, why is she in the shape she's in?"

Nic told Connor the entire story, leaving nothing out.

"It was the most unexpected thing I've ever seen
coming from a woman. It was as if she had no thought of
her own safety. She comes out of nowhere, stabs the one to
my right in the neck with a dagger that she got from God
only knows where. Then without breaking stride, scoops up
the fallen man's sword and levels a man three times her
size."

"Unbelievable!" Connor shook his head in wonder.
The women he knew would freeze in terror, screaming at
the top of their lungs for divine intervention. This action
from a woman was foreign to him, but not unattractive. In
fact, it was quite the opposite. He began to understand the
admiration that he heard in Nic's voice.

Nic continued. "All jesting aside, I owe this woman
my life. She saved me from a lot of pain and physical harm
and almost lost her own life in the bargain. She's tough,
Connor."

"So I'm beginning to believe," Connor said as he closely watched his friend.

"She has a strength I admire. If I had to go into battle, I might want her there with me."

Connor snorted, protesting such an absurd idea. "Have you lost your mind, man? Women don't go to battle. It's barbaric to think of it."

Nic continued to qualify his statement. "Aye, it is, but I'm half-serious. Look, she planned and carried out her own escape, thinking enough in advance to dress and act as a boy. Personally, I think it was ingenious. She was cunning enough to play a mute when I found her so she did not have to answer any questions until we were well past Seabridge's reach."

Connor raised an eyebrow and Nic continued.

"She's exceptionally smart and brave when she manages to get past her distrust, which happens more and more the longer we're together."

Connor nodded, letting Nic talk. His words were quite telling. Connor understood, knowing Nic as well as he understood and knew himself. Nic was falling in love.

Nic continued. "She's pretty in an unconventional kind of way. Not that you can tell right now from all the swelling. I'm not displeased with Henry's choice for me. If I must marry, I really do think she's a good match for me."

She was his from the moment she had awakened in his arms on the side of the road and covered in mud.

"She took a great chance, Nic. Dressed as a boy or not, she must have been desperate to take such a risk. Where was she going?" Connor ventured.

"My thought is she may have been trying to reach London and the king. She was quick to point out the night at the inn that she wanted something from me just as I wanted something from her. Perhaps she saw a way to have me take her to London in safety, and she would be my squire on the way. I got what I wanted, and so did she."

"But you said you were heading north and she agreed to go. It was only after the brush with the search party that you decided to go to London. Are you sure this is not just some young woman's ploy for the attentions of a guardian who's careless?"

"Nay. She never blinked when I told her I knew she was the Duchess of Seabridge. And she was quite serious in saying he'd kill her if I sent her back. I believe her, Connor." Nic took a long draw from his wine. He was worried. The loss of blood was deadly and had left her more fragile. The fever was under control, but that could go either direction very quickly, too.

"She'll always carry the scars both physically and emotionally," Connor was saying, mirroring Nic's thoughts exactly.

"I know. I fear so, as well. Just add them to Brentwood's ledgers. Those were his men." Nic finished his wine. That fact only gave credence to her saying that Lester would kill him, too. That was the intention of that group.

"How can you be certain? They nearly killed her." Connor rubbed his jaw in thought. "However, I can see where he would gain if highwaymen killed the both of you." Connor poured them another goblet of wine and went to stoke the fire to life again. "You're sure those were his men?" he threw back over his shoulder while he stoked the fire.

"Aye, I'm certain they were his men. I overheard one telling the others to 'find Morgan.' I don't believe they were deliberately trying to kill her. I think they didn't know she was going around the countryside disguised as a boy. She was wearing one of my hooded shirts, so they had no way of knowing that it was Morgan. I feel certain the man would not have fought with her had he known."

Connor nodded. "They were expecting a young woman, not a squire. She's tall enough to be successful with the ploy." Connor could see where the confusion had almost cost the duchess her life.

The two men sat in silence for a few moments as the fire crackled and popped. Connor was the first to speak again.

"Does she know about Henry's decree?" Connor watched Nic's reaction.

Nic shook his head.

"When are you going to tell her?" Connor asked.

"Tell her what? That once the wedding has taken place I'll have to take her back to Seabridge? I know I must tell her soon. I had wanted to take her to London and deposit her in Henry's care before I leave to make the necessary journey home. But she can't stay in Henry's care indefinitely, and I must see her settled before I leave for my lands in the north. Seabridge is the most logical place." What was implied was Nic would clean the castle of any threat before leaving her. And that leaving her wouldn't be permanent. He had decided he would try and build a life with her after all.

"Will she be agreeable to this, do you think?"

Nic shrugged a wide shoulder. "I must marry when we get to London. What other choice does she have other than to agree?"

Nic understood that as a woman her choices were few. The king had decreed she would become his bride so she would become his bride. She could do worse for a husband than him, but aside from that, she needed a protector. His gut was telling him Lester Brentwood would kill her if she didn't marry him. Maybe Morgan knew that her death was a foregone conclusion if she stayed behind those castle walls.

~*****~

Morgan backed farther into the shadows. "I've more choices than you could possibly know," Morgan whispered to herself.

She had heard all she needed to hear. Nic had lied to her, and she was surprised at how much it hurt. Yet she had to face the facts that he was going to take her back to Seabridge once he married his woman who was waiting for him in London.

She wouldn't go back. Nic simply didn't understand and obviously hadn't believed her when she said that Lester would kill her. Her heart hurt even knowing his betrayal wasn't fully intentional. She had to get to the king, and it was now or never for her to make her escape.

Back in the sleeping chamber, Morgan quickly gathered her belongings. Feeling guilty but seeing the necessity, she took Nic's coin purse and the small knife that he always kept close at hand. It was all the protection she would have. It was better than nothing. She would repay him once she was able to get her hands on her funds.

Slipping out and into the darkness, Morgan made for the stables. It was harder than she thought it would be to slip past the groomsmen. There was still considerable activity in spite of the late hour. Seeing her opportunity, she slipped unnoticed into the stall where Salt stood munching on fresh clean straw. She had little choice but to risk the ride with only a bridle and a blanket. The saddle was proving to be too much for her to secure and she abandoned the effort.

Just when she thought she wouldn't have an opportunity to get out of the stables, much less the castle walls, a commotion ensued as two men approached the gates demanding entry in the name of the king.

Morgan held her breath as the gates lifted, admitting the king's men across the bridge.

"Watchman, keep the gate open just a bit longer. We have two more coming. They're not far behind." Morgan heard them shout as the party rode into the courtyard, giving her the diversion she needed.

On Salt's back, she slipped past the men and headed east into the night. Spurring the animal on through the darkness, she slumped over on the horse's neck, her body screaming in pain. As she feared, while she was attempting to saddle her mount, the wound had ripped open.

Suddenly she was floating, rising above the pain. She didn't feel or see the blood steadily streaming down her arm as it soaked into the dark woolen cape. Even with a foggy mind, she knew there was something wrong as her disconnection grew. Giving in, she slipped into the blackness closing in around her, which was darker than the night.

Chapter 20

The king's men arrived at Featherstone with orders for Nic and Connor to report to the king at once. They had spent the balance of the night in discussions with Henry's men. Nic was aware that Henry had some trouble brewing in Ireland, and the king needed the services of his two best men.

Nic cursed his luck. Morgan was nowhere near ready to travel, and Nic knew he dared not leave her here to her own designs. He might be away for months, and he knew she wouldn't be here when he returned. She was too much of a flight risk, not to mention still in grave danger.

For the first time Nic's heart was refusing to answer the call of his king. Torn between his responsibility to Morgan and his duty to King Henry, Nic was searching for a balance. He was squarely in that place he never wanted to be.

Nic figured eight days round trip to London and back to Featherstone. Then another four or five to take Morgan back to London. The plan would mean twelve days of hard riding, but it was plausible.

"Connor, I have to leave tonight and go to the king."

"Are you going to ask Henry to delay your deployment?"

"Aye, long enough to get Morgan feeling stronger and safely deposited into his care. I don't dare leave her here."

Connor started to protest. "She'll be fine."

Nic held up his hands in a gesture to stop him from commenting further.

"Nay, don't take offense, Connor. She's willful and fully realizes the extent of her danger. Fear is a very motivating factor, and she could prove slippery."

"She's too weak to cause much trouble at the moment," Connor said.

"Aye, but given a week, I'm afraid she'll have your household up in arms."

Nic's words couldn't have been more prophetic.

~*****~

Finishing the business with the king's messenger, the men began to complete arrangements to leave. All Nic lacked was his knife and coin bag and to tell Morgan goodbye. Upon entering the room, he knew she was gone.

"Bloody hell!"

He rushed out of the room and bolted down the stairs.

"You two search the castle for my squire!" he commanded, pointing to a set of soldiers sitting at a gaming table. Then he rushed out the door, going straight to the stables. Throwing the doors wide, he saw Vernon neatly in his stall. Right next to Trojan was Salt's empty stall.

"Nay even a week to cause this much trouble!" Nic said to his horse. "Now we've a mess," he said, running his hands through his hair. He didn't need this kind of problem.

He should have known better; however, it didn't make any sense to Nic that she would run. Behind these fortified walls, it would take a small army for Brentwood to reach her.

He now had a serious problem on his hands. His king was expecting him in three days and he had a runaway bride to deal with.

Promptly making his way back to the house, Nic gathered three men along the way and found Connor giving orders to his steward.

"What's wrong?" Connor saw the tightness around Nic's mouth, which never boded well.

"Morgan is not upstairs and her horse is gone."

Connor stared at him in disbelief, then shook his head. "And it only gets better, Nic. Brentwood and his men are at my gates."

146

They needed to find her and fast. She was outside the castle walls and was in no shape to survive if she began to bleed, if her fever rose, or if she came under attack. Any and all were possibilities.

Connor placed a hand on Nic's shoulder in a show of solidarity; he knew the situation was critical.

"Nic, we must leave soon. We cannot disobey a royal command, no matter the personal cost to us as men. We don't have much time, but we'll do what we can in the time we do have. Come, let us rally the men. She probably slipped out when Henry's men came in and the gate was open."

"So she has several hours on us at this point," Nic reasoned. "Which might be good given Brentwood is bellowing at the front gates."

"She's probably headed for London, and we are, too." Connor said, hoping that was the case. "Worst case, we ride ahead of the others."

Connor and Nic made their way into the bailey. Brentwood and nine men were waiting at the gates. He was being detained and not happy about it.

"McKinnon, I demand you return my niece immediately! I know she is here," Brentwood yelled.

Nic was in no mood. "Go to hell, Lester." Nic was impatient to begin the search. The longer they delayed, the farther she would be from them.

"I have legal right to her," Lester proclaimed, having no idea the thin ice he was treading.

Nic saw the evil lurking below Lester's surface and knew this man was the cause of his bride's insane bid at her freedom.

"Nay, you don't have any right to her, not any longer, ya sick bastard."

"You will deliver her to me at once," Lester demanded.

Nic was quick to counter that command.

"Not on your life would I deliver that girl back into the care of the likes of you." Nic didn't want him to know he was making a run to catch her. The less the bastard knew the better.

"You'll regret this, McKinnon," Brentwood spat as he pulled hard on the horse's bit, making the poor creature's mouth bleed.

"Not today and never tomorrow. Now, get out of my way."

Lester made an aggressive move toward his weapon. Nic was faster and he pulled his sword. The point pressing to Brentwood's chest was only a fraction away from piercing his black heart. "Dresden, escort this pile of horse manure and his men to the western edge of Holden land. Kill them all if Brentwood so much as acts like he's going to resist," Nic commanded the captain of the guard.

"Aye, sir. It will be our pleasure to escort him off the property."

"You're a dead man," Brentwood said with a hiss as he turned his mount and headed out the gates, accompanied by three dozen of Connor's best men.

Already mounted to ride, Nic, Connor, and a party of six turned their horses east into the morning sun to begin their search.

Chapter 21

It didn't take long for them to find Morgan, for she was no more than a mile from the castle. Nic saw her first and thanked God. They easily could have flown past her, never expecting her to be so close. Morgan's crumpled body had pinned Salt's reins beneath her, and that one lucky move was the only thing keeping her and the animal close.

Nic spurred Trojan into a faster pace, leaving the party behind. Coming to an abrupt stop, he leapt off his horse, just feet from where she lay motionless, facedown on the grass.

Since the night had been very cold, Nic braced himself for the worst. She was alive, but burning to the touch. Nic knelt down on one knee and picked up her motionless body just as Connor arrived and dismounted.

"Is she alive?" Connor asked grimly. He feared the answer.

"Aye, but barely. She's burning up and she's lost more blood. Here, hand her up to me. And let us pray to God it's not too late," Nic said as he mounted Trojan again.

Connor handed her to his friend. Leaning down to receive the bundle his friend offered, Nic felt a rock in the pit his stomach. Again, he had failed to protect her. If she died, it was his fault.

Once they were back at the castle, Connor dismounted first and took Morgan very gently from Nic's arms. Turning to make his way back inside, Nic stopped him. If she died, it would not be in any arms except his.

"Connor, give her over. She's my mine to protect. For all the good I've done."

Connor studied his friend and realization struck. By God, Nic wasn't just falling in love, he already was in love with this woman.

They reached the room, and Nic placed her on the bed, then sat beside her in the chair that he had occupied the days before.

"Bring the priest and do so quickly, Connor. She needs him to pray for her soul. It can't wait." The words almost stuck in Nic's throat.

Connor turned to go but stopped in the doorway, turning to his friend. "Nic, she needs to hear your voice and feel your strength. Don't give her up for dead." Seeing that he wasn't getting through to Nic, Connor tried another approach. "Nic, when have you ever given up what belonged to you without a fight? If you love her, brother, then fight for her."

Nic just looked at Connor as he turned to do his bidding.

~*****~

Connor's statement got him to thinking. Did he love her? In his mind, Nic admitted that he had grown to care for her. How that happened, he didn't exactly know.

Was it because the king had given her to him, and she belonged to him as Connor had implied? She was his possession, and therefore, that is why he cared? No, he doubted that was all there was to it. Morgan wasn't a woman any man would ever fully possess or control. Nor should a man want to control her. He knew controlling her would destroy the essence of the real woman.

He loved her spirit, her grit.

Nay! his heart was screaming. *You love her, period.*

It hit him full force. He did love her. Body and soul, he loved her. For so many years, he built walls, keeping those who pursued him at bay. It had never occurred to him he could fall for the one woman who wanted nothing more than to get away from him.

150

He studied her; she was dying. There was no refuting it. It was in God's hands, and he prayed for the first time in more years than he could remember. His prayers were awkward and rusty but sincere. It shamed him that he had so deeply neglected this aspect of his life. Perhaps his God was forgiving.

Looking down at her gray, ashen face with the bruises still very vivid, the helplessness he felt was overwhelming. He loved her and he was losing her.

He wouldn't let that happen. If she lived, he vowed he would set her free. That freedom was something she was willing to die to possess. He would marry her and leave her to live her life unencumbered. She would be safe from Brentwood and any other predator who might think to possess her for the land and wealth she would bring to them. She was worth so much more than just the title, and she deserved a life on her terms.

The priest quietly entered with Connor just a step behind.

"Father Francis, thank ye for coming," Nic said, standing to greet the spiritual leader of the people of Featherstone.

Father Francis came to the bed and began to pray for her mortal soul. Suddenly, Nic stopped him.

"Stop, Father, nay not yet. You'll marry us first."

Father Francis stopped and looked at Nic. The idea was outrageous to the priest. "I'll not do this act of abomination. It's not proper for a man to marry a boy. The church will never approve and even if I'm quite liberal in my thinking, neither do I."

Nic was livid. "I can assure you, Father, the church will approve. Now, do it before it's too late!"

Connor came quickly to the side of the priest.

"Father, it's all right. Morgan is the Duchess of Seabridge. She is disguising herself as a boy."

"Ah, I see," he said as understanding dawned. "Son, I understand what you're doing here. In light of Lord Brentwood's untimely visit, I see where you should marry her in all haste. It would be valid in the eyes of the church. However, it wouldn't be legal without the proper documentation. That could take days. If Lord Brentwood carries legal rights, then it would do no good."

"Are you referring to this documentation, Father?" Nic pulled the papers from his pack and handed them to him. The papers had none other than the king's own seal affixed.

"Are you going to marry them or not?" Connor asked flatly.

"Aye, I'll marry them," the priest agreed.

This couple was ordained to marry by no less than a royal decree. However, he should not have been surprised. Nic and Connor were Henry's favorites. These two young men were his favorites too. Connor and Nic called him father. He felt it an honor.

"Get on with it," Nic commanded, taking Morgan's right hand in his.

As Father Francis began the ceremony, Nic stood beside the bed of his bruised and battered bride. If she didn't live, he would be able to hold Seabridge legally. Henry could then appoint someone who was worthy because Brentwood would be dead within the week. Nic was going to see to that task personally.

The priest began.

"Sometimes the Lord calms the storm and sometimes the Lord lets the storm rage and calms the child. Bidden or unbidden God is always present. Amen." They all made the sign of the cross. There was no time for a full mass.

"I am going to perform a ceremony that I witnessed years ago. Eventually it will be the norm," the priest said, feeling confident in the statement. "Do you, Sir Nicholas Galen McKinnon, take this woman to honor, cherish, and protect with all that is within you? Do you vow to keep her from harm and raise her above all others for she will become one with your flesh, one with your heart, and one with your soul? Do you promise to look to her happiness? Do you vow to show devotion to her in sickness and in health? And do you vow to do so until your life leaves this world for the next?"

"Aye, I do vow. And should she pass before me in this life, I shall hold these vows sacred and binding until my soul rejoins with her in the next."

Nic took his Christian cross from around his neck and took Morgan's lifeless hand into his. He then placed the only piece of jewelry he owned in her palm, gently closing her hand around it. "All that I am and all that I have, I give it to thee."

Connor's surprise was total. He could hardly believe what he had just witnessed. Nic had just bound himself to the duchess in life and in death.

"It's done then. Congratulations, Nic. You're now the Seventh Duke of Seabridge."

Nic now had a wife and it felt right that it was Morgan. He would have no regrets of this marriage, not today and never tomorrow.

"Shall I pray for her soul now, my son?" Father Francis stared at the large warrior gently holding the dying woman's hand and waited for an answer.

Nic looked at the priest, then back into his wife's face. "Nay. My wife will live." It was a declaration. He would fight for her when she couldn't fight for herself.

Nic turned to Mary, the housekeeper. "Bring me blankets, cool fresh water, beef broth, candles, a bath and a clean nightdress for my lady."

Nic turned his full attention on Connor.

"Now, my friend, take this marriage contract to the king and tell him I have a wife to save if he wishes those future generations of loyal peers to the Tudor crown."

~*****~

"Mary, please summon the healer," Nic asked the housekeeper after she brought the items he requested.

Mary turned to do his bidding, leaving him alone in the room with the woman, who moments ago, became his wife.

"You must live, lass. You're a fighter and will pull through this, Morgan," he said holding her hand, lacing his fingers through hers.

Nic believed his words. He had to believe them. The alternative was now unthinkable.

Chapter 22

As the day dragged on and the noon meal followed, Nic waited for hours for the healer to make his appearance. When he arrived, Nic immediately noted his filthy appearance, refusing to allow the man to be near or touch his wife. He reeked of human and animal excrement. Nic's first thought was they can all go to hell before this man touches my woman.

Nic wondered why people couldn't see the importance of keeping themselves clean. Even he, a mere soldier, knew that there was greater risk of infection in a dirty environment, regardless of what the custom might be. Going against the norm, he bathed regularly and had never been ill a day in his life. In his mind that debunked the theory that bathing was dangerous and sinful. He certainly smelled better than the other men and women who tended to use powders or bags of sweet-smelling herbs to mask their stench. It was rarely successful.

"Sir, you'll not touch my wife until you bathe and place clean clothes on your person, you boggin dunderheed!" Nic ordered the man, not prepared to take no for an answer.

"I will not!" The healer objected, horrified at the notion. "And, ye sir, cannot make me. It's an abomination to wash. Any godly and pious person knows this. Besides, it's obvious to me that she'll die. I say we need to call the digger so he can have her place ready."

"You will not speak thus around my wife!" Nic came around the bed to stand his full height in front of the filthy medicine man. "I'll not stand for it! She'll live and you'll not be here to say otherwise. You'll get out this instant. Out! Out, you filthy bastard. Else I'll throw you from the window slit like the contents of a chamber pot!"

Nic took a step closer to him and the man ran screaming from the room. He nearly ran Mary over in his haste to leave as she was coming down the hallway.

Mary walked into the room, not a bit afraid of Nic. She noted him sitting by Morgan's bed. She came to him, and in an uncustomary gesture of familiarity, placed a hand on his shoulder.

"I know of another. Shall I have him summoned?" she asked softly.

Nic was sitting with his elbows on his knees, his face resting in the palms of his hands. He ran his hands over his face and through his hair. He was at a loss. He was used to fixing things. He fixed the king's problems with the unruly. He fixed disputes between his men, but he was unsure how to fix this. He wasn't in control and it was unsettling. Moreover, he was feeling his own mortality for the first time in his life.

"Aye, I'm willing to try anything. I would even sell my soul to the devil if necessary. Mary, I can't lose her. I think every breath she takes for herself she also takes for me." Nic let out a long and anguished sigh. "Aye, go find your healer."

Mary squeezed his shoulder in understanding. "In the meantime, don't sell anything to anybody, in particular the devil," she said, then turned to leave to find the healer.

~*****~

As the hours passed, Morgan's condition grew worse, something Nic hadn't thought possible. Having to physically restrain her as her fever soared, he feared she wouldn't make it before the second healer arrived.

At last, before dawn, the second healer arrived, making his way to the bed to inspect Morgan. He was clean. Nic had Mary to thank for that blessing. The man touched Morgan's face and looked at Nic, completely devoid of

156

emotion saying, "I can heal her, but I must have privacy for my administration."

"Nay," Nic said emphatically. "I'll not leave her alone with you."

Nic didn't want to leave her alone with this man. He left Nic with a cold, unsettled feeling. He couldn't quite put his finger on it, but there was something dark and evil about this healer. *Perhaps he's Druid. After all they still exist in secret*, Nic thought.

"We have no more to talk about." The healer turned to go.

"Wait. All right, I'll leave, but not for long."

Nic didn't feel good about leaving but would leave if that was what it would take for the man to help.

Fifteen minutes later, Nic silently entered Morgan's room to find a scene that struck horror to the very depths of his soul. The man was chanting in some unknown tongue, and he had opened a wound in her wrist allowing her life's blood to drip into a bowl.

"You're bleeding her? Get out!" *Not again*, Nic thought.

The man jumped, spilling the precious contents of the bowl, splashing Morgan with her own blood. Nic grabbed the man by the collar and threw him out with such force the man slammed into the far wall of the corridor. Nic closed the door, bolted it, and refused to let anyone in for hours.

~*****~

Over the next few days, Nic allowed no one else to touch her. He cleaned her, bathed her with cool water when her fever soared, prayed, and repeated the cycle. He held her when she was delirious with fever and screaming from nightmares. He wasn't so sure they were not memories that she was reliving in vivid detail.

He gathered her near and rocked her. It seemed the only way to calm her when the terror visited her.

"Morgan, it's all right, lass. I'm here. Stay with me."

Morgan was calmer and her breathing steadied. He held her and rocked her more.

Sometime later as the evening moved into night, Nic fell into an exhausted sleep, cradling her in his arms. Near dawn he woke covered in sweat. Her fever had broken sometime in the night as he had held her close. Touching her forehead, her skin felt cool and dry. Her breathing was steady and her sleep was natural and deep. She had survived this round. Nic was overwhelmed with relief.

"Thank you, good Lord, for her life. I promise to do right by her," he said, voicing his prayer and vow out loud.

Nic eased Morgan out of his arms, then covered her with the sheet and quietly left the room.

It had been eight days.

~*****~

Nic made his way downstairs to the kitchen after leaving Morgan's room. The kitchen was warm, bright, and smelled of freshly baked bread, which was a relief from the smell of the sickroom.

The cook was surprised to see him.

"How is she?" he asked, fearing the worst. Everyone in the household knew that Nic hadn't left his lady-wife for days. That act alone spoke volumes to all of them. Morgan was more than just wife to this young man whom they all adored as much as they loved Connor.

"She'll live," Nic announced, then grinned about the good news.

"Oh, that is wonderful news. I'll go tell Mary. Should I have her help ye with Her Grace?"

"Aye, please. I'm starving and need to sleep. Please ask her to come up as soon as she can have a meal and a bath made ready." Nic grabbed a roll from the counter as he made his way out.

~*****~

Not long after he bathed and ate the meal Mary had brought him, Nic crawled into the bed next to Morgan and slept soundly for hours. When he woke, it was dark outside and candlelight softly danced from the single flame. He had no idea how long he had slept, but the rest felt good and revitalizing.

Morgan was still sleeping. He took the opportunity to look at her through the candlelight. He brought her hand to his lips.

"You're going to be fine, Morgan."

When she was stronger, he would give her freedom. She had been ready to die for it. He felt his heart hurt, but he had promised and he was a man of honor.

Chapter 23

The chambermaid brought in a tray of food for Morgan to eat. Nic gently shook Morgan to wake her.

"Morgan, you need to eat something, lass."

She opened her eyes and looked at Nic, then closed them. He touched her face with his fingertips.

"Morgan, you need to let me help you sit up to eat, love. I promise you may sleep once you do."

Morgan opened her eyes again, taking in her surroundings.

"I thought I escaped or was that a dream?"

Nic shook his head. It hadn't been a dream but definitely a nightmare.

"Nay, not a dream. You tried but only got outside the gate."

"I feel like a newborn kitten, and I had the most terrible dreams. I thought I was back at Seabridge," she confessed.

"You've been sick nine days, lass, and almost died." Nic paused. "I'd not let that happen. Let me help you sit up."

Placing his arm against her back, he helped her to a sitting position. The sheet fell away to reveal her wounded shoulder and left breast. She grabbed for the cover and brought it to her chin, embarrassed he had seen her.

"Don't feel embarrassed, Morgan. Who do you think's been taking care of you?"

"He wouldn't let anyone else touch ye, Your Grace," the maid said as she closed the door to go get fresh water for a bath.

"I owe you a debt of gratitude. I hope you know that it was never my intent to be a burden to you."

"You're not a burden, Morgan. So, push that thought out of your mind. But one has to ask, what were you thinking, lass?"

"I guess I wasn't, not really, but all I could think was to run."

She couldn't look at him.

Taking her chin, he lifted her gaze to look at him. "Why, love? Why run from safety? Why run from me?"

The question hung heavy in the air, and Nic took her hands in his. Morgan opened her mouth to speak just as a tap came on the door. She pressed her lips together again. Nic waited. Seeing that he would get nothing out of her, he rose to open the door. It was Mary.

"May I help Her Grace in any way?" Mary asked cheerfully.

"Aye, Mary. If Her Grace wishes to take a bath, please help her. I think I've completed my work here for the moment. My men are waiting." He turned back to Morgan. " 'Tis good to see you improved, Duchess." Nic bowed at the waist.

Pulling Mary back out into the hallway, he whispered so that Morgan couldn't overhear. "Don't say anything about the marriage. I've not had the opportunity to tell her. So, please pass this directive to the rest of the household as well."

"Aye, sir." She curtsied and returned into the room.

~*****~

Nic returned to their room after his training practice with the intention of sharing with her the news of their legal contract of marriage.

He found her asleep, looking peaceful and vulnerable; not wanting to wake her from the much needed restorative sleep, Nic decided to join her.

He removed his clothes and slipped into bed with his wife, opening his arms as she turned to him in sleep. He kissed her on top of her head and breathed in her sweetness. He inhaled again deeply, closed his eyes, and gave over to a dreamless sleep.

Chapter 24

"Up ye come, Miss Sleepyhead." Mary burst into the room with her usual merriment and good cheer. "Our dashing knight wishes ye to eat again. Here, let me help ye sit up, me dear."

Mary came over to the bed after setting the loaded tray on the table and helped Morgan to prop herself up in the bed. She was feeling stronger and more herself, and she had Mary and Nic to thank for that improvement.

Morgan looked at the mound of food. "Well, I hope our dashing knight doesn't need me to eat all that. I'll surely explode."

She and Mary giggled at the same time.

"Oh, Duchess, it's so good to see ye feeling better." Mary clasped her hands over her ample bosom and beamed brightly. "The McKinnon will be pleased to see ye today. Your color is improving even from last evening. Now, let me bring ye some food."

"I think I would like to try to sit at the table. Can you help me get there? I'm feeling stronger, but I'm still weak as a kitten."

"Oh, of course. It would be my pleasure."

"Nay, the pleasure is all mine this morning, Mary." Nic had entered the room unannounced. Morgan jumped at the sound of his voice. She wondered how he was able to be so silent when he completely filled the room.

He is so beautiful and larger than life, she thought as his dark hair hung loose and flowed down his back like a glorious cascade of dark silk. His tunic was open at the front in casual contempt for propriety, and the tightly fitted leggings hugged his powerful legs. *There is something to be said for the male form*, she thought. Especially when beautifully put together like he was. He looked as sensual and as unobtainable as she knew him to be.

Seeing him so darkly handsome didn't dampen her mood. She would enjoy him to the very end. She wasn't as uncomfortable in his company as she thought she should be, knowing he had nursed her in her illness. *That had to have been very unpleasant*, she thought, realizing that throwing up on his boots the first day was nothing compared to what he must have seen after her failed attempt at freedom.

Nic sensed the change in her. He wasn't going to let her mood deter him, though. He leaned down and scooped her up, blankets and all.

"Nay, Nic. Please, put me down."

"Verray well, m'lady. I'll do as you command just as soon as I get you to this chair." She had lost weight. At this point his bedroll weighed more than she did, Nic mused as he deposited her in the smaller chair at the table.

Nic was glad she was feeling better, and knowing her as he did, he felt he needed to place some stipulation on her getting up and around.

"I really don't mind seeing you up and out of bed as long as you behave."

"Behave?" Morgan held in a laugh. The idea of her causing trouble was preposterous. She was so weak there wasn't much trouble she could cause. However, his expression told her he fully believed she was trouble incarnate. "I'm a perfect little angel."

"Pffft! A little devil is more like it, and you know it too" Nic came back at her all in good fun. "All jesting aside, you're not to overdo for at least a day or two longer. That's an order." Nic saw the telling sign she was perturbed. "Oh, for heaven's sake, Morgan, sheath the claws. You're verray weak and are not but skin draped on bone. You were deathly ill not three days ago and are still at risk of a relapse. If that happens because of your own stubbornness, then I'll just let you die, thinking you must surely have a death wish."

He should have stopped there, but good sense had fled and was now overrun by frustration and exhaustion.

"And after all, you're the Duchess and therefore, your every wish is most certainly my command!" He did a mocking yet graceful bow from the waist, sweeping his left arm wide in exaggerated gallantry.

"You're being a gallant arse, Nic. Do you think me being 'skin draped on bone' is something that I intentionally did to myself? You think I want to look like a skinny boy? Well, you can blame my uncle for my skeletal state."

He was instantly contrite for his words.

"I'm verray sorry, lass. I shouldn't have been so hard on you, and aye, an arse I can certainly be, but you need to understand that you must take care of yourself. And that begins by eating a good meal."

And to hell with your uncle, he thought. The man was a sword tip away from being a skeleton himself.

Nic served their plates. He hadn't planned to eat with her, but he was going to stay. His men would just have to wait. Morgan looked over at her breakfast companion. Nic had begun to eat and her stomach growled in a most undignified fashion.

He chuckled.

" 'Tis a good sign, I think. Now go on and eat. I haven't saved your life just to have you starve." He was teasing her and she smiled, making him wonder how he was ever going to let her go.

Chapter 25

Nic had found other sleeping arrangements after the morning he had taken breakfast with Morgan. However, he had continued to have meals with her. As they had finished breaking their fast, Nic sensed Morgan wanted to ask him for something.

For her, the days passed with monotony and routine, and she was going crazy. She was feeling much better and needed more activity.

Funny how quickly attitudes change, she thought.

Not so long ago, she had spent years confined by her uncle Lester, yet she never felt as caged as she did, a pampered guest, safely tucked behind the walls of Featherstone. Having tasted freedom, she found she craved it even more.

Morgan cautiously approached him. She was feeling much stronger and wanted to escape her rooms where she had spent the last ten days.

"Nic, do you think it would be possible for you to take me for a short walk outside the castle today? The weather looks to be mild and I'm feeling much stronger."

Nic hesitated, but how could he resist the pleading look that was in her eyes? Lord help him should she ever discover the effects she had on him. He always lost all sense of good judgment around her.

She could probably ask me to jump from the parapets and I would, he wagered with himself.

Closing his eyes, he shook his head at his internal musings.

Morgan thought he was declining her request.

"Very well, I'll not ask again."

She turned away from him, back to the window looking out over the countryside.

Nic moved behind her. Placing his hands on her shoulders, he felt her stiffen. Tenderly, he turned her around to face him, lifting her chin with his hand. Looking into her eyes, he saw her eyes moist with tears, and the idea that she was sad was almost more than he could bear.

"Morgan, you mistake my intent," he spoke tenderly. "I was just thinking how I lose all the good sense God has given me when I'm around you, lass."

As if to prove his point, he stepped closer, taking her face lovingly into his hands, rubbing his thumb across the pink and tender scar on her cheek. Gently, he placed a kiss upon it. He stepped back and let his gaze travel down to her mouth. Her lips looked moist and were slightly parted in mute invitation. Cautiously, he lowered his mouth to hers.

It was a tender kiss, almost reverent, worshipful.

That one small kiss touched him more deeply than any passionate kiss had ever done. It thrilled him to the core, and Nic was reluctant to release her. Slowly, he withdrew his mouth from hers, his hands still framing her face.

"Aye, Morgan, you may have your walk. I'll send Thomas to you."

He kissed her on the forehead and left the room before she could recover.

~*****~

Nic left Morgan in Thomas' care and went straight to the training fields where his men awaited him. He always trained several hours a day, and this day he worked straight through the midday meal, having gotten a later start than usual.

As the day wore on, he became more and more distracted. Consequently, his sparring partner kept landing blows that, under normal circumstances, he would have had no trouble deflecting.

Cullen stopped and studied the man who was as much his mentor as he was his brother. Something was bothering Nic, and Cullen had a few pieces of advice for him.

"Nic, if you're going to train, then train. If you're going to daydream, then get to the gardens," Cullen said, with no malice intended.

His brother's words drew Nic's attention, and he silently admitted, although younger, his brother had a point.

"I'm sorry, Cullen. I guess I'm just a little off center today."

"Look, Nic, you always told me 'never let personal issues get in the way' because it will cost me. Great advice then and still is good advice. Don't let her get to you, brother. At the wrong time those distractions will get you killed. You know?"

"Aye, I understand what you're saying. Is it that obvious?"

"Let me just say that I understand your position. But your situation will work out, I feel certain."

"I'm glad one of us is so cocksure," Nic said under his breath, then looked back at the castle, specifically Morgan's window.

"She just needs time to adjust," Cullen offered. "Let her become accustomed to the idea of being the wife of one of the most feared men in the king's realm. She shall figure out soon enough how to wrap you around her little finger." Cullen laughed, poking fun at his older brother.

"She can't adjust if she doesn't know," Nic said, taking his sword and stabbing the blade into the earth between them. Then he ran his hands through his hair.

Cullen stood with jaw open.

"You haven't told her, and you turned her loose with Thomas? Have you lost your mind? You know Thomas can't keep a secret, Nic. He's not malicious. It's just a byproduct of his never-ending prattle."

Nic began to feel the pangs of panic. What if Thomas slipped and told her of their marriage? It should come from him. He had to tell her soon, but he had been stalling because he was completely unsure of what her reaction would be regardless of the source. And he didn't want her to bolt!

"I have to go, Cullen. I'll see you at the evening meal. If I'm not there then come looking for me. I'll most likely be locked in my bedroom suite with my wife, fighting the battle of my life. She's verray independent."

Cullen laughed, shaking his blond head. "Women." He sobered. "I pray I'm wrong, Nic, but you may not come out the victor on this one, my brother."

"Somehow, I feel you just might be right." Nic turned and headed back to the castle and wondered exactly how he was going to break the news to her that he was the Seventh Duke of Seabridge.

~*****~

In her room, Morgan was studying the training field. She had a good view from her window and from her vantage point never found it difficult to spot Nic.

He was head and shoulders above the rest and always aggressive in his training. Yet while she had watched him, she could see something wasn't right with him. He faltered. She had seen Cullen get in a couple of good blows. Were he really engaged in battle, those blows would have cost him his life.

She saw him stop, run his hand through his hair as he talked with the tall, blond, young man who had arrived at the castle a few days ago. She had discovered he was Nic's younger half-brother. Having watched Nic over the last week, she had figured out that when Nic ran his hand through his hair, he was frustrated and a bit edgy.

"At least I'm not the reason for it," she said as she watched him turn to leave the field.

Morgan shivered. He made her insides tighten in a way she had started to recognize as sensual.

"He's magnificent," she said as he made his way back to the keep. She continued to watch, following his movements until he was out of view.

She moved away from the window and began to ready herself, wondering if perhaps he would take supper with her. She was dying to show off one of the three new gowns that had arrived this morning. She didn't know why, but somehow it felt important for her to dress with care this evening.

Nic had trained through the midday meal, and she found she missed him. He was intelligent and had a sense of humor to mirror her own. They usually found each other's company light and enjoyable. His friendship was easy to accept and hers easy to give.

Apparently, he had put her illness behind him. His behavior towards her was relaxed, comfortable, and anything but sexual. The exception was the kiss he had given her that morning.

She knew he liked her. They enjoyed each other's company, yet it pricked her pride that he didn't think of her in terms of a desirable woman. She guessed it might be different between them if she were tiny, blonde, and curvy. As he had pointed out earlier, she was just skin stretched on bone. She had gained some weight from the food Mary brought to her, and he had insisted she eat, but Morgan knew she was still very thin. Consequently, he didn't look at her as if she were a woman at all.

The realization hurt.

Morgan wished it were not true. However, she was a realist and the reality was this: Nic McKinnon was in love with a woman, and that woman wasn't her.

On their walk earlier in the day, Thomas had told her King Henry decreed Nic must wed and that he did seem resigned to it.

Morgan had to agree. She hadn't heard Nic complain about the royal decree a single time, and if she had learned anything about The McKinnon in the time they had spent together, it was that he was loyal to Henry and would follow the king's decree to wed. However, that loyalty wouldn't ensure he would do so meekly or quietly if it didn't suit his plan or desires.

That brought her to one conclusion: Nic wanted his bride. That left her out of the running, but she could be his friend. Beyond that, she would never have him. She steeled herself against the sudden pain of the realization that once he wed, he would be gone from her life, no matter how much she deluded herself into thinking that they could remain friends.

Morgan had realized something that morning just before he kissed her. Nic could be the one man to steal her heart, and he was the one man she could never have. Deep inside, Morgan already knew she would suffer his loss in her life.

"Nay," she said firmly to the stillness of the chamber. She wouldn't allow any man to have that much control over her. Tomorrow was her birthday. She would be twenty-one and free.

Chapter 26

Morgan dressed with the greatest of care. Selecting and discarding several gowns, she finally chose the emerald green silk, shot through with gold thread. The scooping, scandalous bodice showed off her creamy skin, providing the perfect backdrop for the beautiful cross now hanging from her slender neck.

It was the first time she had dared to wear it.

The rosewood cross and heavy gold chain somehow felt comforting to her as if connecting her to something greater than just herself.

Mary brushed her hair and wove flowers into a laurel with colorful silk ribbons that when placed on her head hung down her back. Nic was thoughtful enough to have a pair of soft kid slippers made for her, which arrived just that morning along with the dress.

Mary stepped back to survey her handiwork. "Oh, child, let me look at ye. Ye are simply a vision. Your skin is back to a beautiful cream, and your eyes are sparkling like emeralds."

Morgan was stunned. No one except her father had called her beautiful, and that was because she looked so much like her mother.

"I thank you, Mary. The dress and headpiece are gorgeous." She smiled nervously at the older woman's appraisal.

"Have ye never been told ye are a vision, child?" Mary saw Morgan's embarrassment and felt she knew the cause.

"Nay. I have always been too dark, too tall, and too flat to be considered beautiful. One suitor called me a giraffe," Morgan said as she ran her hands down her breasts and stomach, feeling very conscious of her height. At six feet, she towered over most men and all the women she knew.

"Oh, that is such nonsense, just look at me. I'm round and short and Thomas thinks I'm beautiful. There'll be others who will think ye beautiful."

As she was leaving, Mary thought there was one knight in particular who would find Morgan irresistible tonight.

Morgan peered at her reflection in the mirror, wondering if Nic would notice her, and questioned why his attention even mattered to her.

~*****~

Mary let Nic know Morgan was ready. He was sitting in front of the great fireplace discussing with Cullen the probability that Henry would soon be calling them to London.

"My lord, she's ready and looks beautiful tonight. I think ye will approve." Mary beamed like an artist unveiling a masterpiece.

Nic tapped lightly on her door before opening it to her soft invitation. He saw her there by the window looking out into the early twilight. Her profile was sleek and graceful. Slowly, she turned to face him. Nic thought Mary had underestimated the effect. Morgan was beautiful, and she took his breath. He had no idea a woman could make him feel so calm, so strong, and so alive.

Nic crossed the room to stand beside her and gallantly bowed. Taking her hand, he slowly brought her palm to his lips, kissing the sensitive spot on her wrist. It was such an intimate gesture that it sent a tingling sensation through her.

"You look beautiful this evening, Morgan. I would be honored, Duchess, if you'd be my companion for tonight's May Day festivities in the Great Hall."

Morgan was surprised. She hadn't dressed for public dining.

"Nic, I'm overdressed for the occasion. I don't want to seem pretentious to our hosts." She felt shy, suddenly aware of how revealing her dress was and realizing with a start that she had dressed for Nic's eyes alone.

"Nay, Morgan, you're perfect. Come with me. Let me have the honor, lass." He crooked his right arm in silent invitation. Smiling up at him, she tentatively slipped her hand into the bend of Nic's elbow; she found he wasn't the only one having problems breathing.

He placed his hand over hers, and they descended the staircase to the Great Hall.

Cullen was standing at the base of the staircase and swore he was viewing a small slice of heaven.

Chapter 27

The feast was wonderful. In celebration of May Day, wine flowed freely and several kinds of meat, bread, and cheese covered the table. Dancing, music, and song brought happiness to the hall, and Morgan enjoyed herself immensely.

Nic watched her closely for any signs of fatigue. All he saw was a beautiful woman glowing with excitement. Feeling satisfied with her reactions to the evening's festivities, he sat through the courses and the early evening with little interest in anything except this vision seated beside him. He couldn't keep his eyes or hands off her, and he felt as if he were a lovesick youth.

Much to his dismay, she was having the same effect on all the men in the hall. She had danced with several of the men, and he was having trouble keeping unfounded jealously from dampening his spirits. She was his and all knew it as a fact, but they also knew he hadn't fully laid claim to her, but that was about to change.

As the evening wore on, Nic excused himself when a messenger arrived requiring his immediate attention.

"Morgan, there's an urgent message from Henry demanding my attention. Please, continue to enjoy yourself. Cullen will be here in a few minutes should you need anything. I won't be long," he said, then kissed her hand before he left to find Cullen.

Nic pulled Cullen aside and asked him to attend Morgan until he returned.

"I'll attend her with pleasure, brother. She'll be far easier to attend than Baron Whitten's daughter." Cullen's dining companion was known for her constant whining, her vicious gossip, and her ill treatment to her household staff. She also had a voice so shrill it raked down one's spine. Her exquisite beauty didn't make up for any of that in his opinion, and he was grateful to have a reason to excuse himself. "Nic, Morgan looks beautiful," Cullen said, and then he looked back at Morgan and let his eyes travel over her. "There's no mistaking her for a lad tonight."

"Careful, Cullen, you tread in dangerous waters, lad." Nic realized almost too late that Cullen was just paying him and Morgan a compliment. "If I see you have designs on my woman, I'll have you married off to Baron Whitten's daughter before sunrise," Nic teased and grimaced for the man who would have her as a wife. Life wouldn't be pleasant. It was common knowledge the Baron's dowry for her was astronomical, yet there had been no takers.

"Nic, do you hate me so?" Cullen asked, wide-eyed in overstated shock. "I always had my suspicions and now I know it for fact," Cullen said with his hand clutched over his heart and exaggerated dismay etched into his attractive face. "You should've drowned me at birth, brother. Drowned me as a bairn to save me from the pain that I feel as a man knowing you so despise me." Cullen finished his monologue with a dramatic flair.

"The evening is still verray young," Nic said dryly, raising one dark brow. "I may yet have time to grant your soulful wish."

Cullen burst into laughter and patted Nic on the shoulder.

"Go on, Nic, the messenger is waiting. I'll be happy to guard your woman as if she were my own."

Nic stood for a moment studying his younger sibling. For a split second, Nic didn't see a brother. He saw him as one male would another. Nic was allowing Cullen into his territory. He prayed his brother's motives were pure, for all their sakes, as he went to meet the messenger.

Fifteen minutes later, Nic had confirmation. It was as he feared. Henry was out of patience. He and his men were to report immediately, no excuses, no reprieves. He returned to the Great Hall as Cullen was seating Morgan.

"Cullen, we need to talk," Nic said grimly.

"The news is not good?" Cullen asked as he stood by Morgan's chair.

"Nic?" Morgan asked in anticipation. Was this the news she was dreading?

Nic laid a reassuring hand on her shoulder, and she automatically reached up to cover his fingers with hers.

"Nay, not good, but not unexpected either. The king has grown impatient, and we're to report to London without further delay. Cullen, you need to ready the men. Aaron has the orders. Report to him. Give him what support he'll need."

"Aye, sir." Cullen was in military mode. "When do we leave?"

"We'll leave at dawn."

Morgan watched as the two men talked. These two were so alike, yet so different. Cullen's light hair and eyes contrasted Nic's dark olive complexion. In profile they looked strikingly similar, and when they faced forward the family resemblance was even stronger.

She knew they had the same father but different mothers, yet Nic treated him as total blood. They had a close and genuine relationship.

"Is it known?" Cullen asked cryptically.

Nic knew exactly what Cullen was talking about, Morgan was sure.

"Nay, but soon. If you will, please excuse us? I need to speak privately with my... with Morgan." Nic turned to Morgan. "Duchess, I'll walk you back to your chamber where we can talk in private."

Nic excused them from the guests and guided her silently upstairs to their chambers. Morgan watched his body language. She was becoming a master of reading his ways.

He has something on his mind, she thought.

Nic had to tell her he had married her. He would tell her that he would personally see to Brentwood's elimination before he left for Ireland. He would tell her she would be free to live her life the way she wanted to live it.

He would have his own life back, too, but was that what he really wanted now? He thought not. When he looked at Morgan, he saw his future. He could picture his children and a good life with a good woman. Knowingly or not, Henry had chosen him a fine wife.

He held the door for her and after she passed through, he softly closed and bolted it behind them. For the first time in many days, an uncomfortable silence hung between them. He had to tell her tonight. They were leaving tomorrow.

Lost in her own thoughts, Morgan knew after tonight he would be forever beyond her reach. He was leaving tomorrow. This would be the last opportunity for her to be with this man as friend or lover. She wanted to take a piece of him with her to face her unknown future. This one piece would have to last her a lifetime.

He was on his way to London, to his king and his bride. He would take her to London until he married and then deposit her back at Seabridge on his way to his ancestral home. Or perhaps if she asked, he would leave her here at Featherstone to her own designs. She wasn't sure what would be the worst form of torture: never seeing him again or going to London with him and seeing him married.

Tonight was all that mattered. All she wanted was to kiss him again, to touch him, to feel him.

He wasn't totally indifferent to her. He had touched her hand, stroked her thigh under the table, and whispered closely into her ear all evening.

She, somehow, felt that she should feel shame at her thoughts, but she didn't and what was more, she wouldn't. She had long ago learned to take life's pleasures when and where she found them. Tonight was all she would have, and she would take what fate would allow her.

She walked to the table and poured a single goblet of wine. She turned and closed the space between her and Nic.

He stood by the fireplace wrestling with his own demons of how to tell her.

"Morgan, I need—" Nic lost all coherent thought when he turned. She had loosened the lace openings down the front of her gown, which gave him a tantalizing glimpse of flesh.

"You have need of what, my lord?" The undercurrent of her words was thick with sensuality. With both hands around the goblet, she lifted it to her lips and drank. Turning the goblet around so his lips would touch where hers had been, she demanded, "Drink."

Any thought of talking about the marriage ended as he took the goblet to his lips and drank from the communal cup.

Morgan took the goblet back and sensually licked a tiny droplet clinging precariously to the rim. She had no idea what that did for him. She nearly drove him over the edge with the tiny flick of her tongue.

Taking the goblet from her hands, he set it down and knew their talk would have to wait.

He had only one thing on his mind: laying siege.

~*****~

Just before dawn, in the bed where he had made good his threat of siege, Morgan watched Nic sleep. She had never dreamed of pleasure with such heights or pain of such depths.

He was leaving her today.

Tenderly brushing a lock of hair from his handsome face, she looked down at her lover and spoke softly in the coming dawn.

"You're a thief, Nic, and it's my heart you have stolen. Now I know what might have been but can never be."

If she had doubts about loving him, she doubted no more. She loved this man with everything in her soul.

For her there could never be another.

Chapter 28

May 2, 1493

"Happy birthday, Morgan. Follow your heart."

Morgan hovered in the clouds of light sleep before her eyes popped open. Her mother's voice came in the times of her greatest need. She had stopped trying to figure out the phenomenon and just accepted it.

The first time she heard her mother's voice was the morning of the fire. The duchess' voice had awakened her. Maybe true love was stronger than life or the grave.

The house hadn't arisen as yet, but she got up and calmly packed, being careful not to wake Nic. She had come to a decision and her mind was set. She would beg him to take her to London. It would grieve her to see him pulled from her by the king's demands, but she had to talk to King Henry.

Maybe she could get her audience and be gone before Nic ever exchanged his vows. She felt her heart begin to die at the thought of him being forever out of her reach.

"You're up early," Nic purred from the bed where they had spent last night locked in passion's embrace. "Come back and let me welcome the morning properly with you, lass."

"Nic, please allow me to continue on to London with you." Morgan tried her best to sound calm, but her voice was strained. The thought of going back to Seabridge was unsettling. "Please, I beg you. Don't leave me here. I have to speak with the king."

Nic threw the covers back, revealing the evidence of their union, the blood smeared crimson on the linens. He padded in all his naked glory over to where she was standing.

God, he is glorious, she thought. With his hair flowing, his body iron hard and firm as steel, he was completely at ease with his state of undress.

"What kind of greeting is this? No 'good morning'? No 'last night was wonderful'?" He teased as he reached for her.

Sidestepping his attempts to touch her, she wouldn't let him distract her from her purpose.

"Nic, I'm serious. I'm not letting you leave me behind this morning. If you leave without me, I will only find a means to get to London on my own."

Nic knew she was serious. He pulled her to him in a reassuring embrace. He placed his chin on top of her head and ran his hands up and down her back. She was stiff and unyielding.

Nay a good sign, Nic thought.

"You're going with me to London. That has never been in question." He pulled back to look into her worried face. "Morgan, of course, you'll come. Why would you think I would do anything except take you with me? I had planned it all along. Besides, do you think for one minute after what we shared last night that I'll have you anywhere except close to me? I want you even now, and it hasn't been an hour since I made love to you." He kissed her on the top of the head, thinking the subject closed. "However, I'm late and need to get dressed, but you, my lovely lady, have been the most exquisite reason I have ever had for being late to guard call." He turned her loose and continued reaching for his clothes.

"Take me for the right reason, Nic, or I go alone," she said as Mary knocked on the door, bringing in a tray of food.

Morgan hadn't given thought to what the house servants might say or think if Nic was still here this morning. However, Mary didn't seem surprised or shocked that he was there. In fact, she seemed pleased to find him naked too.

Too late now, Morgan supposed. Besides, she had things of much greater importance to deal with this morning than what the house staff might or might not think.

Nic turned back to Morgan as soon as Mary left.

"All right, Morgan, what is on your mind?" he asked as he buckled on his sword. "Why would you think that I wasn't going to take you to London for the right reasons?"

"Because you really want to take me back to Seabridge. Is that not your ultimate plan?"

"Aye, I do and aye, it is. However, not today. Did I say I'd not send you back to Seabridge? I understand such a move would put you into grave danger. That's something that I swore to avoid at all cost. You're verray important to me."

Nic was now in full warrior dress. Morgan couldn't help admire the aura of power and strength he exuded. He was magnificent. Her mother would have said he was a gift from the Goddess of War, yet after last night, she would argue that Nic was a gift from the Goddess of Love.

She shook herself, knowing she needed to get off the treacherous path her heart was taking her and answer his question about the night she ran.

"After I recovered from the fever, you asked me about the night I ran." Morgan walked to him, her arms crossed over her chest. "You asked me why I would run from safety, run from Featherstone…"

Nic interrupted and finished her sentence. "And why you would run from me? So—now am I to get the why of it from you, Duchess?" Nic asked.

He was afraid he wasn't going to like this answer. Crossing his arms over his chest, he mirrored her stance, not realizing how intimidating he appeared.

Morgan stood her ground.

She took a deep breath and continued. "That night I fell back to sleep after you left me and when I awoke, I came looking for you. You had said you would be downstairs talking to Connor."

"And?"

"And, I went down the stairs and saw you and Connor by the great fireplace. I swear, I wasn't purposely eavesdropping, but I heard you talking. You said you were taking me back and that you knew I couldn't stay with the king indefinitely. You said that once you were married you would see me deposited back at Seabridge on your way home. I assumed you would be taking your tiny, blonde, and beautiful new bride with you and deposit me on the way past."

"Och! Mary, Mother of Jesus, Morgan, you heard only part of a conversation. And what do you mean tiny, blonde, and beautiful bride? All you got right in that sentence was the bonnie part."

He was dismayed to hear her confession of overhearing the conversation. What else had she heard? He was trying to remember. He had said something about the marriage and, oh God, he could see where she would think he had a bride waiting in London and she would be deposited back at Seabridge. That was why she ran.

She didn't trust him to keep his word. He had said he wouldn't send her back, and she didn't believe him. That hurt even if he could see where she might have thought differently.

"And last night," he asked. "What was that to you, m'lady?"

"The same thing it was for you—memorable."

"Somehow I doubt we're of like mind on the subject."

She had said she wanted last night to take her through all her tomorrows. Had she thought last night would be the only night they would share together? Had she thought him so insensitive and of such a nature to take a highborn virgin

188

when he had a bride waiting? Did she think he would share with her the most devastatingly passionate night of sex he had ever had, only to leave her for another? What else must she think of him?

"You're way off course on this one, lass. You only heard part of a conversation and have no idea what's in my heart, Morgan."

"Nay, I know exactly what I heard. I have to get to London, Nic." Morgan continued, her voice rising, "I wasn't going to allow you to take me back to Seabridge then, and I certainly will not be forced back now."

He grabbed her gently by the shoulders. "Morgan, calm yourself." Nic was beginning to find the situation anything but amusing. "You're right. You won't go back today. Nevertheless, go back you will when the time is right."

"Nay, I won't, and you along with the whole of the king's army can't force me either."

"I'm not arguing with you about this, lass. It's pointless. Seabridge is your home. It belongs to you, and you have every right to be there and to live free of fear."

"Nay, McKinnon, I won't go back. Not until I speak to the king. He has to remember the agreement with my father."

"Agreement?" That stopped Nic in his tracks. "What agreement, Duchess?"

Nic felt something shift inside. Agreements between kings and upper-crust noblemen were common enough. What if Henry had agreed to give her to another and had forgotten? The thought was unimaginable to him now.

"In return for my father's backing for Henry's crown, Henry agreed that if I reach my twenty-first birthday unwed, then Seabridge and my person will be returned to my care alone to manage as I see fit. Today is my birthday, Nic. Do you not see? As of today, Seabridge is mine and mine alone. My uncle no longer has power over me."

"Really? No man has any power over you, you say," he repeated, his words dripping with extreme cynicism.

"I answer to no one except God and King Henry."

Nic was taken back at the implication of this agreement and the direction Morgan was heading with it. It was obvious to him. She didn't intend to take a husband. He was on very shaky ground where she was concerned and needed to regain his composure.

"Morgan, think for a moment about what you're saying. Why would the king give up a prime piece of land to be managed by a slip of a girl?"

"He agreed," she countered.

Nic shook his head. "Women and land are a means to an end. You know this and know that I'm right. In addition, I know Henry. He would never agree to such a thing. This practice is not done, Duchess. Land and marriages are rewards and used to build and strengthen alliances. And, even if he did sign it, Henry is king. He can change his mind."

"But—" Morgan started to speak, yet Nic held up his hand instantly silencing any argument she might have had.

"And while we're on the subject, let us talk, shall we, about your uncle for a moment. What in God's name makes you think a man like Lester Brentwood would walk away just because his niece has reached adulthood and says so? Do you think you'll simply walk into the Great Hall and announce you're the duchess of the castle and he'll acquiesce to your wishes and give up all he feels he has rightfully earned?"

"Well, I think—"

"Whatever you might be thinking, it's unrealistic," Nic interrupted. He had to drive some sense into her while he still had the time. "Morgan, men like Brentwood don't give up without a fight, and that fight is usually dirty. You need a husband. You're vulnerable without one and wrong to think otherwise."

Morgan was livid. "And you think I'm not just as vulnerable with one? You think I need a husband? Why, Nic? So he can lock me in the tower for weeks on end with nothing but a moth-eaten blanket to keep me warm and just enough wood for a fire to burn for one hour a day? Or beat me senseless because my French is a bit accented. Or wait, what about this one?" She fired sarcastically. "He could lock me in a rat-infested, spider-ridden cellar for a week with no candles. Why, Nic? Please just go on and tell me why I need a husband. Perhaps, so he can push me aside once I give him his precious heir? His heir to the land and all that goes with it that is rightfully mine? He would be my husband, so who would be there to stop him? You? The law? Society? All would say it was his right as my lord and husband to do with me as he saw fit. And it's you who's wrong to think otherwise. No, McKinnon. No! I don't need a husband and I don't need you. I will get to London on my own." She wheeled to get her pack to leave.

He saw where this argument was heading and pushed past her to block the door. Nic thought she would have fought to the death if the need had arisen.

"Out of my way, McKinnon. I'm exercising my options. This is the door I choose to walk out of and the time I'm choosing to do it."

Nic dared not budge. For a brief moment, he felt fear she would do exactly that. She might just walk out and never look back.

He took several deep breaths before continuing in hopes of defusing the predicament. If he had told her last night that she already had a husband, then none of this would be happening. He certainly couldn't tell her with her in this current emotionally charged state. *She just might make herself a widow,* he thought, somewhat amused.

"Nay, I can't allow you to leave me, Duchess, and I'll not argue with you about this, either. You're not going anywhere without me beside you. I said that I'm taking you to London, and I'll do just that. Let me get our trunks together, and we can take it one issue at a time. Agreed?"

She didn't back down and continued as if he hadn't said a word to her.

"I wish to borrow a complement of men from Connor. I will gladly pay for their services. However, as you are fully aware, I currently don't have the means at my disposal, but I do have the funds. You can go to London unencumbered and answer your call to arms." She stopped for a moment in her request to give greater weight to her final words. "And, Nic, you can also go to the devil or your bride. I don't care which." It was a lie. She cared deeply.

"At the moment, I believe my bride and the devil may be one and the same."

Nic could see that Morgan didn't understand his retort, and that was just as well. Nic was beyond furious, and he wasn't just late to muster the men, he was very late to get them assembled for the journey to London.

"Fine, Morgan. You'll get your men. They'll take you to London and escort you to the king. I'll ride ahead and give Henry fair warning of your impending arrival."

Nic was two steps from losing control. His fear was he would do her harm if he stayed any longer, only giving credence to her argument of an abusive husband. Instead he marched over to where she had rooted herself, crushed her to him, gave her a brutally passionate kiss, turned and left the room with a stunned Morgan in his wake.

Chapter 29

"Women," Nic mumbled as he went down the stairs in search of Aaron, his master guardsman. Cullen was with Aaron, and Nic drew his brother to the side and out of earshot of the others.

"Trouble in paradise, Nic?" Cullen asked, sensing Nic wasn't happy, and his guess was a tall, beautiful, dark-haired woman was involved because the servants were gossiping about how Nic had spent the night with Morgan.

"Cullen, do not tangle with me this morning. I still might drown you for it." He ran his fingers through his hair, a sure sign to Cullen that his brother was frustrated. "There has been a change in the plans. I need you to gather our most trusted and loyal men. Form an escort for Lady Morgan. I'm placing her life in your hands. I don't trust anyone else except you for this task. Do you understand?"

"Actually, nay, I don't understand." Cullen was trying to go through the reasons why Nic may have made this request. There wasn't a single one that made sense.

"She has refused to allow me to take her to London." Nic lowered his voice. He didn't want the men to know his woman had refused his protection. He would never live down the insult.

Cullen began to protest. "How can she refuse? You're the best person for the job. And—"

"I know! I know!" Nic interrupted, lowering his voice. "Nevertheless, it must be done as she wants it. I'm afraid she'll make the slip if she feels she's not in complete control of these particular circumstances."

"Why will she not allow you to escort her, Nic?" Cullen asked.

"She doesn't trust me." Nic's simple reply was unexpected.

"Why on earth would she not trust you? Did you tell her, and that's the reason?" Cullen was searching to understand why Morgan was so mistrustful of the one man Cullen knew to be the most trustworthy.

Nic was beginning to be uncomfortable with the direction the conversation was heading. "Ah, nay, it never came up."

"What do you mean, 'it never came up'? I thought you went upstairs with the purpose of telling her."

Nic was beginning to feel ashamed. He had let the passion between them detour him from his original purpose.

"I hadn't planned on staying the night, Cullen. I was going to tell her and leave or at least let her make the choice. I just ended up with more pleasant things to occupy our time, and this morning she came at me first thing with talons bared."

"You're a bad liar, Nic. So fool yourself if you want but don't try to fool me," Cullen said as he pointed at his older brother's chest. "You had every intention of claiming Morgan when you shut and bolted the door to her chamber last night." He didn't even wait for Nic to try and deny what they both knew was the truth. "You married her and she has a right to know. You've failed her and you know it."

"On several levels," Nic admitted.

"You know the Code of the Knight. 'To do an action is to own that action.' It's your action to own, Nic."

"But—"

"I've never said this to you before, but you're dead wrong on this one, my brother. You're wrong to keep her in the dark as long as you have. She deserves better than this and well you know it."

Nic knew Cullen was angry and this made him feel worse. "Just get her safely to London. If I'm still at court when she arrives, I'll tell her at that point."

194

"Well be warned, Nic, if you're gone when we arrive, I'll tell her. We can't leave her in the dark and certainly not at Henry's court. She would feel like the laughingstock of the realm if she finds out by other means. She has pride, Nic. It would crush her, and if you think she doesn't trust you now…"

Nic bristled. "Well… Have you not just become the expert on my wife's feelings?"

"Now you're being an arse. You're her husband for Holy Christ's sake. It should come from you, but if not from your lips, then at least it needs to come from family," Cullen retorted, feeling beyond irritated with his older sibling. The man had certainly gone soft in the head on this one.

"Verray well, you tell her if I have already left to join my troops."

"Nic, are you sure you really want to do this?" Cullen gave him an inquisitive look and a final chance to back out of leaving Morgan in his care.

"Am I sure? Nay, I'm not sure about anything when it comes to my woman except that she means a great deal to me. Keep her safe at all costs, Cullen. You'll have to watch her like a hawk, too. She can be slippery, and there is still danger lurking out there for her. I have no idea how Brentwood will act once he realizes she has slipped from his grasp." Nic placed his pack on the back of Trojan.

"I'll defend her with my life, Nic," Cullen vowed. "She's worth it."

Nic was looking at his younger brother. Was he wise or just a bit in love with Morgan? Who would blame him if he were?

"No one, and I mean no one, is to touch her, understand me? And should she ever doubt I care for her, just tell her I love her more than my horse. She'll understand."

With those parting instructions, Nic mounted Trojan and headed east to London, to his duty, to his king.

~*****~

Morgan stayed in her room during all the preparation for departure. She would have been in the way had she tried to help. Standing at the window, she watched the love of her life ride away from her.

It's best this way, she kept telling herself. *This will make it easier,* she thought. It had to make things easier because she was dying inside. He had gone and she had driven him away.

Yes, it was best this way, she repeated, as she shed tears for herself, for him, and for the life they would never share.

~*****~

Stewart watched as the party made ready to go. He watched Nic ride out ahead with too many men for him to be waylaid. He turned his attention to the lady. He knew after last night things had changed.

Undoubtedly, so did the rest of the castle. Her husband had staked his claim, and the lady hadn't objected. Brentwood's chances of securing Seabridge were growing slimmer by the day, and there might well be an heir already on the way. However, there always was a way around most any problem. The key was to know just how far a man was willing to go to solve that problem.

He chuckled. He was the kind of man who usually had no boundaries, and this time was no exception. He smiled bitterly as he watched the Duchess of Seabridge mount up to ride. If he had his way, the little witch would soon be back in the tower room just where she belonged.

Chapter 30

London
The Royal Court

Nic was true to his word. Riding ahead, he notified Henry
and the queen of Morgan's pending arrival.

The apartments Morgan found herself in were opulent
beyond her wildest expectations. She had never expected
the king to place her in such lavish surroundings as she
currently found herself in. It didn't dawn on her that the
rooms and accommodations were customary and befitting a
duchess who was also a distant relation.

The outer chamber was large and spacious. The stone
fireplace, set into the corner, blazed with a welcoming fire
even though the days were getting warmer. The dining
table was graced with silver candlesticks holding expensive
scented beeswax candles, and a writing desk complete with
ink and parchment. There were also several chairs
embellished with embroidery so fine it had surely taken
years to complete a single cushion. The hunt scenes were
miniature masterpieces with stitching so fine Morgan had
to look closely to even see them. The fur rug in front of the
hearth was sable, soft and luxurious to the touch. The
lovely purple cloth covering the window slits was heavy
velvet, trimmed with gold brocade. The tassels had fine
beading of pearls, gold, and silver. A serving set consisting
of a jewel-encrusted wine decanter and two matching
goblets sat on the table between the two chairs in front of
the fireplace. The small parchment announced the serving
set was a gift from the king.

Her bedroom wasn't as large but instead had a feeling
of intimacy. The floor was covered with soft rugs
throughout the room that padded her feet no matter where
she walked. The fireplace had a set of chairs strategically

placed, and they begged for intimate and romantic conversation.

However, it was the bed that dominated the room. It was set at an angle in the far corner, and the linen canopy draping it was the most beautiful material Morgan had ever seen. The sheerest white fabric gave the illusion the bed was floating. It captured the firelight, reflecting the light— like a hazy, warm mist. The bedcover and pillows matched, and Morgan found she wanted to burrow into the lush linens, letting the feel of them take her mind away from Nic and how much she missed him. It was a bed made for love. She wouldn't have recognized it for what it was a fortnight ago; however, after spending that one wonderful night with Nic, her eyes were opening to a new and remarkable world. Her nights in this beautiful room filled her with deep and desperate longings. The bed felt like it was crying out for two.

She had barely left the chamber since arriving, and she hadn't seen Nic in ten days. She knew he was here and missed him dreadfully. After being away from him, she hated thinking how desolate life was going to be without him.

The last ten days were torture when she let her mind drift to how they had parted at Featherstone. Angry words had severed them, and her need to apologize to him was eating at her. He was her friend, and she wanted to ask for forgiveness for her behavior. She had thought that by pushing him away it would make her inevitable loss easier. But doubts had crept in, knowing at this point nothing would ease the heartache sure to come with his pending nuptials.

Cullen made it clear on the trip from Featherstone to London that she had hurt Nic. She had not trusted him to keep his word, and his word was his honor. Cullen said that Nic took responsibility seriously. Morgan was his responsibility. Yet she had thrown his offer of protection back into his face.

Seeing her behavior in retrospect, she realized she had acted horribly, but her actions and words had come from fear and pain. But that didn't make it acceptable. She would ask him to forgive her if she had opportunity to see him. She had already written him a letter and asked Cullen to deliver it to him. He assured her the task was completed.

As the days moved forward, Cullen kept her informed, and she knew Nic was there but still in closed-door sessions in the war room with the king and his advisers. No one came in and no one left without the king's permission according to Cullen.

Morgan thought about what she had learned about Cullen, a young knight as honorable as Nic.

Len, as he was known by a few close friends, was wonderful company and the perfect escort for her trip to London. She was finding she liked him very much. His sense of humor was wonderful, his company companionable. He would make a wonderful husband someday when the right woman came along. He was definitely handsome and would become more so as he matured. He was attentive, and even-natured, with a mind just as intelligent as Nic's.

On the journey to London, they had talked at great length. Morgan discovered there were three boys. Brandon was the oldest, Nic the middle, and Cullen the youngest.

Cullen stated that as the youngest of the three, he didn't have to deal with the rigors of life because he grew up with two older, more formidable brothers. Therefore, he hadn't had to shoulder the weight of much responsibility.

Morgan doubted he was irresponsible and said so. She told him that false modesty was unbecoming in McKinnon men and that there was no use in trying to hide their competencies. She said Nic must have figured it out because she had never seen even a hint of humility, false or otherwise, in him.

Cullen had laughed. There was no sense in denying or admitting the truth about Nic or himself. The truth was that Nic had no time for modesty, and Cullen was capable of handling great amounts of responsibility.

Currently Cullen was handling the greatest responsibility ever handed to him. Nic trusted him to lead the team responsible for the safety of the duchess.

He didn't have to deny or admit it to her because Morgan saw that the men followed him without question, and that didn't happen simply because he was Nic's brother. Cullen was competent and intelligent, and he possessed a code of honor and principles by which he lived. The men respected him, and it wasn't fear driving these men to follow as it was with her uncle Lester's men.

He was a knight who earned his spurs three years earlier after foiling an assassination attempt on Queen Elizabeth's life. Since then, Morgan was sure his deeds of valor were great if unsung.

Cullen shared how Nic joined the service at an early age to have hope of becoming successful. He had climbed the ranks quickly. Morgan had no doubt about that truth. But she was surprised to find out that he was knighted at seventeen for his bravery on the battlefield where Henry won his crown. Nic's prowess was legendary according to Cullen. Morgan didn't doubt that, either.

Cullen on the other hand had inherited land from his mother, Heather Williams, who was the second wife of his and Nic's father, Patrick McKinnon. Cullen was wealthy and landed in his own right.

Brandon, the oldest brother, was fifteen years Nic's senior. There were two other brothers and a sister in between, who had never made it much past early childhood. While Brandon was still alive, he managed the land for Cullen. He was just five when his mother passed away, and far too young to manage the estate on his own. The land he had inherited butted up to the McKinnon ancestral home, so it was convenient for Brandon to merge with Heather Park and run it as one large estate.

Cullen had just never seen any reason to change things, so he joined with Nic several years ago. Cullen liked the arrangement. He was Nic's man and Nic was the king's.

Thinking of Nic, Morgan walked over to the dresser and pulled out the lovely nightgown she found on her arrival. She rubbed it to her cheek, its softness a thing of wonder to her. It had been in a box on the bed with an envelope with her name in handwriting she recognized as his. Few knights were literate, yet the fact Nic could read and write wasn't surprising. He understood the importance of the written word.

She ached to see him; however, if his betrothed was here he would be paying court to her. Morgan felt seeing Nic would probably never happen. At least that meeting wouldn't happen in private.

And Cullen had told her Nic would be on his way to Ireland soon, gone for months. Could he already be gone? Surely, he wouldn't leave without saying goodbye. Had her words driven a wedge so deeply that he wouldn't say goodbye even for the sake of their friendship?

Still holding the gown in her hands, she wanted to see how the fabric would feel next to her skin. She undressed without help and slipped the nightdress over her head. The garment skimmed her body in a slow caress of silk, reminding her of Nic's fingertips.

"Do you approve, Duchess?"

Nic had never seen anything more beautiful than Morgan at that moment. He thought he had died and gone to heaven as he had walked into the room just in time to see the silk from the Far East shimmer past her shoulders, slender back, and bottom as it molded her as a second skin.

His timing had been perfect, for he knew she couldn't have known he was coming.

Morgan whirled to face the man of her dreams. "You came to me," she whispered, her words filled with soft longing.

She was glowing as he crossed the room as quickly as his weary legs would take him.

She met him halfway and he crushed her to him. "God, Morgan, I have missed ya, lass."

She placed her forehead on his chest and began to pour out her heart. "Oh, Nic, I have missed you, too. I'm so sorry and ashamed of the way I behaved and for what I said. I was scared and I should have trusted you. Can you ever—"

Nic shut off her apology with a kiss so deep, so full of longing, she was lost in it and never wanted to be found. How was she ever to live without him?

"I feared that you were already gone," she confessed.

"I swear, love, I would have come to you before now, but I have just been given leave by the king."

"I greet you with arms that have been empty and a heart that has felt lost." Morgan felt the words deeply, Nic sensed the truth in them, and they touched him to his core. She cared for him. Could she love him?

"Oh, Nic, I have missed your touch and kisses, but I have longed more to see you, to talk with you, to fellowship with you as my friend."

"I'm here now."

"How long?" she asked. However long it wouldn't be enough.

"We have tonight. Let us make the most of it." Nic held her close, breathing her in. "I have to leave before dawn, even though it's not my wish to do so."

"What of your betrothed?" she asked innocently as he leaned in for a kiss.

Nic hesitated, his mouth hovering just above hers. The moment had come. Nic knew he couldn't avoid the issue any further. He hesitated, torn between telling her now or telling her after he had made love to her.

Morgan saw his hesitancy and took the decision out of his hands.

"We'll speak on it later," she said, brushing her lips softly against his neck.

Nic pointed to the bed, never taking his eyes off the vision in front of him. "Call me shallow, but right now, I only have a single thought on my mind. And that is to make love to you in that bed until I have to be carried off tomorrow on a litter."

Morgan giggled as she took his large hand in both of hers and in a mute invitation walked backwards, leading him to the bed that cried out for two.

Chapter 31

As they lay twined together, serenity wrapped them in a blanket of comfort. They had come together the first time hard and fast, both just feeling the need to satisfy the desire brought on by the absence of the last weeks and the emotions pent up from wanting each other.

The second time Nic savored her like a fine dessert. He had made love to her tenderly and thoroughly with his body and with his words. They undeniably felt the bond between them strengthening. Lying there in the room made for lovers, they were in their own world where none could touch them and she wouldn't think of tomorrow. Tonight wasn't enough, but it was more than she had ever hoped to have with him.

Nic held his wife, absently stroking her back and hair, thinking of how much he loved her. She had become his friend, his strength, his reason for living. He had fallen hard for her, and he was hopelessly at a loss to know what to do to make this right.

He knew he was about to hurt her, and the truth tore at his insides. He had felt that he was doing what was right at the time by marrying her, and he still felt he had made the right decision, but he hadn't asked what she wanted. She came to London asking to exercise her right to run her lands and property on her own. Yet from the beginning, Nic knew Henry would deny her that right. Sharing his concerns, Nic conferred with the king, presenting the contract held by the Sixth Duke. Against his better judgment and certainly against his heart, Nic petitioned Henry to speak to the pope about annulling the marriage and for Henry to grant her sovereign right to her lands. It wasn't what he really wanted, but he felt it was what she wanted. Nevertheless, the king, being a man as well as king, sympathized but wasn't about to get involved in the annulment of a legally binding marriage consummated freely by both parties. Besides, Henry had cautioned him about approaching the current sitting pope. Alexander VI was born in Spain as Rodrigo Borja of the influential Borja family. He was a corrupt, worldly, and ambitious man of dubious spiritual and ethical character who might grant the annulment but would certainly extract an extremely high price to obtain it. Henry had advised him to leave it alone and not to draw unwanted attention to Morgan or himself from the papal direction.

Henry didn't deny the agreement that was made with the Sixth Duke of Seabridge. He just wasn't inclined to grant an unwed woman sovereign rights to her lands and thereby set a dangerous precedent. Henry sent Nic away with a pat on the back, congratulating him on having a beautiful, rich, and intelligent wife.

Nic agreed that she was all that and more. He just was at a loss as to how to tell her.

~*****~

Morgan knew Nic was awake. He was running his fingers through his hair, and more than once, too. He was thinking, that much she knew. About what, she couldn't tell.

Morgan broke the silence first by trying to ease the tension she felt beginning to rise from him. "Want to talk about it?"

He sighed and she felt the romance flee.

"Morgan, love, we do need to talk."

She raised herself from his shoulder where she was lightly running her fingers through the dark hair on his chest. "Nic, what is troubling you? This is serious, is it not?" she asked. Looking into Nic's face, she saw just how serious he was at the moment.

"Aye, it is. I'm afraid there's nary a way around the fact it will change both our lives for better or worse. Come, let us get dressed and move to the fireplace. I don't want to discuss this in bed."

"All right, if that is what you wish," she said, beginning to rise.

"Wait."

Before she rose, Nic took her in his arms and kissed her with all the love he felt for her. If this was going be the last time he was with her, he wanted all he could get. He needed to show her how important she was to his very existence.

Yet, as much as he wanted the feelings to linger, the talk could no longer wait.

Chapter 32

Watching Nic dress, Morgan felt a terrible dread settle in the pit of her stomach.

For better or worse, he had said.

She was betting on worse.

Pouring them both a glass of wine, she sat down in one of the chairs in front of the low-burning fire. He walked to her chair and crouched down in front of her. Taking the wine from her hands, he set it aside. He took both of her hands into his and gazed at her. Silently, they looked into the depths of each other's eyes as Nic tried to collect his thoughts and figure out the best way to broach the conversation.

"You're killing me, Nic. Please, just get it over with."

She thought she knew what was coming. He was going to tell her about his marriage, and she had steeled herself for the emotional blow. Still, knowing it was coming didn't make it any easier.

Nic hung his head. He couldn't look at her. He hung his head, not from shame, but because her face was so open and full of trust, even when she knew it wasn't going to be good news. And he was about to shatter that trust.

Finally he looked back at her. She deserved his honesty.

"Morgan, first of all, I want to tell you that I have grown to love you deeply, and I wouldn't change a single act I have done when it comes to you, love. Everything, all of it, I did because I felt it was right. I still feel it's right. I love you, deeply, and I wouldn't change one second of the time we have shared in the privacy of this bedroom or the one we shared at Featherstone. I want you desperately, and I know that will never change. However, I'm afraid your feelings will be different when I'm done. I want you to try to remember my words, Morgan. I'd not go back and do anything differently, nothing."

"Nic, what are you trying to say? This has to do with your marriage?"

"Aye," he said flatly.

"Nic, I understand the fact you are getting married. The king has demanded you wed, and you're a man of honor. You have no choice. I know that. Therefore, we have no choice. I may not like it, but it's a fact I have had to face no matter how painful. I know we only have what time remains before you speak your vows, and I will take what time we have left together. And, I will cherish it for the precious thing it is."

The moment was on him. There was no more time.

"Morgan, I'm already wed."

The silence hung between them as Nic saw her eyes growing bright with unshed tears. Suddenly one slipped over the rim. Nic watched it fall in slow motion. If she had only known it was his undoing.

"Nay, please God, tell me this is not true," she said breathlessly. "I had hoped for more time. I had hoped... So this is goodbye. I will miss you."

She began crying softly as she threw her arms around his neck.

"Morgan, look at me, love," Nic said, uncurling her arms from around his neck. Taking her hands to his lips, he kissed her fingers. "This is goodbye only if you wish it, but if I have my way, we'll have all the time in the world to be together once I get back from Ireland."

Shaking her head, she couldn't think in those terms. "Nay, Nic, we don't. I'll not be your mistress. It wouldn't be fair to your wife or to me."

The decisive moment was on him, and he knew the next words out of his mouth would change their worlds forever.

"Morgan, love, you are my wife."

She sat in shock, unable to register the four small words he had just spoken to her.

"You are my wife," he had said.

She shot up out of the chair and moved behind it, placing a barrier between them.

"How dare you play with me," she cried out in protest.

"It's no jest, Morgan. I'm your husband and you are my wife."

"You will explain this in terms that are clear and concise. I will have the truth!" Morgan was angry. Her world was spinning out of control.

Gently, Nic tried calming her. "It's your right, Morgan, to know the truth. Therefore, I'll give you the truth. I know that I should've told you sooner, but the time never seemed right. I'm sure seeing how upset you are that I should've told you the moment you were conscious and let you deal with it as best you could." Nic took a few tentative steps toward her and continued. "For God's sake, you almost died on me. I felt you needed to be stronger. I wanted to tell you before we left for London. I came upstairs with you to tell you the night I received Henry's summons. It was wrong not to tell you, and I was selfish and got distracted by the night we had together. I should've told you sooner."

"What have you done?" She was panicking, and instinctively, she already knew.

Nic wanted desperately to go to her. Knowing it wasn't wise to try to touch her, he just gave her what she asked for and had deserved to know long before now.

"After you ran that night, we found you the next morning in such a state that we all felt you wouldn't survive. You'd lost so much blood and the fever was raging in you. We held out little hope for your living through the day. I had Connor call for his priest to pray for you. As he was leaving to go get Father Francis, Connor said something to me that got me to thinking. He asked me when had I ever given up anything belonging to me without a fight. Well, you belonged to me, and I was going to fight for you. When the priest came, I had him marry us. You were mine by right. I had the king's decree, and I knew if you died without that marriage, Brentwood would have gained the prize. I didn't want him to win because you would not want him to win. I married you to be able to have someone there worthy of it." He took a long draw off the wine and continued. "The cross you wear is my wedding gift to ya, lass. When I placed it into your hand, I realized I was not going to let you die. It was unthinkable to me. I made a promise to God for saving your life, Morgan, and I intend to keep it. I knew you were running from something or someone. I figured that someone was Brentwood and that something was captivity. You ran from me, too. You were willing to die for your freedom, so I gave it to you."

She didn't know what to think. On one hand this was exactly what she wanted. On the other, she hadn't been given the choice.

"So… Tell me just so I'm clear: how exactly do you think you gave me my freedom by binding me in a marriage that you know I never wanted?"

"I had plans on disposing of Brentwood and then leaving you at Seabridge to do as you please. My name would always protect you. You'll no longer be a pawn or be in danger of being forced into an unwanted marriage."

Morgan was amazingly calm considering she had just been told she was married with no knowledge of the action. "Nay, no, I suppose not. How could I possibly be forced into an unwanted marriage when the deed has already been done," she retorted. Yet, somehow it didn't ring quite true. "I thought I knew you, Nic. You deceived me."

"Morgan, you do know me. I won't be cruel to you. I won't lock you in the tower room or in the cellar. And since you already have a husband there can be no other. The king will not allow it, nor will I. I made a promise to you, and I'm prepared to let you have your freedom. The marriage will stand, so the only thing to do will be to let you live your own life free of me. I have already asked the king to speak to the pope on our behalf for an annulment, but Henry has refused since we freely consummated the marriage."

"Well, at least one of us was freely consummating a marriage. I was just being a romantic little fool." Then what he had said sank in. "You are seeking an annulment?" she asked feeling shock and even more wounded by the situation.

"Aye, yes. But it's not my true desire and an annulment is most unlikely to be granted. I'm especially thankful it won't be given your uncle's disposition to violence. There are ways we can work this out to your satisfaction and keep Henry happy with the situation." *Not that I'm happy about leaving her,* he thought.

"So you're leaving me at Seabridge and going about your merry way? You're free to go about your business unfettered by a wife. Yet, I on the other hand am not free."

"It's what you wanted," Nic countered.

"Nay, Nic, it isn't. I would sit behind walls of stone year after year in a castle I despise, and you dare to call that freedom? Nic, you have accomplished nothing because after ten years if I have no children, the king could marry me off again, anyway. Unless we have children, your gallant gesture is for nothing, and at this point, it's very probable we'll never have babies because I wouldn't let you near me if my life depended on it!"

Her defense mechanisms began failing her for the first time in years. Her chest felt tight, her head pounded, and pulse raced. As she looked at her husband, realization dawned.

The silence was deafening as Morgan walked over to Nic. Crossing her arms, calmly and slightly, she cocked her head to the side.

"I was the *nasty business* you were coming to take care of at Seabridge before heading to your home in the north."

"You were to be my bride. I was on my way to claim you."

"Tell me, McKinnon, exactly when did you realize I wasn't a boy?" She needed the total truth from him.

"It's of no consequence when I figured it out."

"Who are you to say it's of no consequence? It's of consequence to me! When, Nic?"

"Morgan, will you please just let it go?" Nic asked.

"Why should I let it go? When?" she demanded.

"From the moment you gave me your name." Nic's flat reply couldn't have hurt her any more.

She looked into his eyes. Yes, she saw remorse. She didn't care if Nic had finally decided to confess or that he was sorry.

She felt like the fool in a game she would never win. And for the first time in her life, Morgan knew bone-deep resentment. She felt resentment for being a woman, resentment for her parents dying, resentment for her king not living up to his word, and resentment at her husband for not being honest with her.

"You knew and you played with me. I guess you felt that was for my own good as well?" She didn't wait for an answer, already knowing what the answer would be. "So, you were on your way not to claim Morgan Pembridge. You were on your way to lay claim to the prize I was to give you. The reward was the title of Duke of Seabridge and all the spoils for your honorable and faithful service to our king. You were on your way to claim a piece of land. You couldn't have cared any less about the woman behind the walls." Morgan's heart hurt.

"Morgan, how was I to know you would be so perfect for me?" Nic asked, knowing she was hitting very close to the truth of that day on the road to Seabridge.

"You never had any intention of living with me, did you? You were on your way to your lands in the north when you found me. You said you had nasty business to attend to before continuing north. You were going to marry me and then go on your merry way. Therefore, either way, you get your freedom. I bet you're sorry you married me since I lived." Morgan let the tears softly flow, making no attempt to stop them.

"Do not speak thusly," Nic said as he pulled her into his embrace. "I'm verray sorry our marriage happened the way it did, but I'm not sorry for the act. That, Morgan, I'll never be."

She eased out of his arms. Nic felt her slipping away from him.

"Nay, I'm sure you aren't. Why should you be? You have total and irrefutable claim to one of the largest and most prosperous dukedoms in the entire king's realm. You're an extremely wealthy man because of this joining of our bodies. For a second-born son with no prospects of land of his own, this is quite a coup, would you not say, my lord?" There was one last questions burning for an answer. "Who else knows of our marriage?"

Nic didn't answer. What could he say?

"So, that's how it is. I'm the last to know."

It was a statement, not a question. Once again she began to pace the room, and then she stopped and slowly turned to face her husband. "You asked me to trust you, McKinnon. I did. Such the fool I have become. You have taught me a valuable lesson today. I guess I should thank you."

Nic saw her erecting emotional walls around her heart, the drawbridges lifting and the portcullis descending. Not only was she emotionally slipping away from him, but he was losing her. He walked over to her and placed his hands on her stiff shoulders.

"Morgan, I leave in hours. Please don't leave it like this between us. There's much to talk about. We need to settle where you will stay until I get back. You're my wife and I want you somewhere safe. I could be gone for months." The silence was drawing out between them. "Morgan, please, say something."

She stepped away, tears of agony and betrayal streaming down her face. Reaching up, she pulled the cross off her neck. Taking his hand, she gently laid the cross into his palm. Had it been a dagger, he would have taken it and pierced his heart, so great was the guilt that he felt.

"Morgan, forgive me."

"Nic, you just don't see. It isn't a matter of forgiveness. That you already have from me. It's a matter of trust." She paused, not knowing what to do next. "Your men are waiting," she said after taking a deep breath for courage and strength. "Go."

Holding that symbol of his promise to protect and cherish her, his clenched fist dropped to his side. He studied her face as he would any opponent for any sign of relenting. When he saw none, he knew retreat was his only option. He had lost the battle and wasn't so sure he hadn't already lost the war.

"Nic, I need time," Morgan said, knowing that commodity was all that stood between her and total heartache.

"As you wish, my bonnie lass," he said, quietly giving her a sweeping bow and gently closed the door behind him.

She felt her world collapse on her as the latch quietly clicked shut.

Chapter 33

"Cullen, you must stay here and keep an eye on her. I've hurt her deeply," Nic confessed. He could no longer hear any movement through the bedroom door as he had when he stood in front of it during two previous attempts to talk to her.

"I told you so," Cullen said, hating to be the one to say he told him what was going to happen. Cullen knew Morgan was the one to suffer for it, and over the last few weeks, he had come to care for her a great deal. "So, Lady Morgan didn't take kindly to being played the fool?"

Nic nodded. "Nay, she didn't. I'm afraid I may have lost her. She erected defenses around herself which have been honed from years of practice, and unfortunately, I'm not in a position to lay siege to her and dig in for a long campaign to win her back."

"Well, at least the truth is out in the open, and she'll come to terms. Morgan is intelligent and she does care about you. You'll have to give her time, Nic."

"That's what she asked for. She trusted me, Cullen, and I threw that trust away." Nic ran his hands through his hair again. "Will you stay?" he asked Cullen. "I know guard duty isn't what a young man would like in a detail, but I have need of a trusted man to keep her safe."

Cullen shrugged as if it were a foregone conclusion. "She's important to you. So I'll stay. Nevertheless, I would've stayed anyway, even had you not asked. She's important to me, too, and I'm well aware of the dangers still posed to her. You have no choice but to go. It's logical that I stay behind and watch the lass in your stead."

Nic began to scowl at his younger sibling. He had never experienced rivalry with Cullen before, but he wasn't going to leave Morgan in her current state of vulnerability so a man could take advantage of her. In addition, Nic knew she liked Cullen a great deal. She may love him as her husband, but understandably, she didn't like him at the moment.

"Now, pray, Nic, don't look at me like that. Aye, I love her, but not as you love her. She's your wife. We're family."

Nic surveyed his younger brother's face and saw nothing there to give him pause, and at this point, Nic had no choice. His king had called him to arms. Morgan could not come with him. Leaving her behind was the only option he had available to him.

Nic tried the outer door to her chamber and found it unlocked. A wave of panic struck him hard and he began thinking she had fled the castle. However, as he looked around, he found her things were still in place and the tray of untouched food sat where it had been placed.

She must have let the servants in to deliver the food and failed to bolt the door behind them. For so many years, she had others locking her in, and it must not always occur to her to do the locking herself. He made a mental note to tell Cullen to watch for that.

He saw her bedroom door ajar and quietly made his way across the room to see if by chance he could have one last chance to talk to her. He hated leaving with things as they were between them. Expecting another bout of words with her, he slowly pushed open the door. He didn't see her at first. Then he spotted her on the floor by the fire.

Nic smiled ruefully. *Things have come full circle*, he thought, kneeling down and carefully picking up his exhausted bride from her pallet. He gently laid her on the same bed on which he had declared his love to her.

Maybe it was not too late for them. Quickly, he drew out parchment and ink and followed his heart.

Morgan,
My Wife, My Heart, I love you.

Remember my words: I would do it all again.
Nic

He placed the note on the pillow next to her. It ripped at his heart to know he was the cause of her distress. Maybe he would do it all again, but he certainly would do it differently. Cullen said she would see the light, and he had to have faith in Cullen's words.

Quickly, Nic pulled off his cross and put it next to the note. Lovingly, he brushed her locks back from her forehead as he leaned down and kissed her tenderly.

Standing beside the bed, Nic wondered if he would ever see her again. It had never bothered him before to go do his duty for his king. It never occurred to him he had any reason not to go. He knew that he had no choice other than to answer his king's calling, so go he would. However, now he had a reason to come home. As he looked down at his sleeping wife, he vowed to return to her.

Cullen was waiting for him as he exited the private chamber.

"She's sleeping. I didn't wake her. Make sure she locks her door, Cullen. She doesn't think about it. This is twice that I have been able to walk into her room unannounced."

Cullen nodded.

Nic looked back at the closed door. "I have to go. I can't delay any longer. The men are waiting."

"Good luck and Godspeed. You take care of yourself. You have a wife to come back to now."

"I have to go, Cullen." Nic gave the door one last look. "Guard her well. She has become my world."

"Just give her time, Nic. Just give her time." Cullen smiled at his brother as they clasped wrists. Pulling Cullen to him, Nic gave Cullen a hearty hug and left him standing outside Morgan's door.

~*****~

In the outer bailey, Nic's men were standing ready for his order to move out. He was making his way to Trojan when he swore he heard someone calling his name in the distance. Did he dare hope Morgan had come to see him off?

Turning, he saw Lady Elizabeth, one of the king's wards, rushing toward him. In total abandon, she threw herself into his arms and unashamedly kissed him full on the lips. Nic pulled away from her.

"Oh, Nic, I just couldn't allow ye to leave without saying goodbye. I love ye, and I will wait for ye to return, I promise," she said with great show of feeling and a little tear for the dramatics of it. Nic didn't see her look past him and smile in satisfaction.

He quickly pulled away by taking a single step back but left his hands resting on her waist as a way to keep her from closing the gap. He looked down at this beautiful, young woman and thought how foolish she was. Not long ago he had fully taken what she was freely offering.

Nic had found through his twenty-nine years the only constant in life was change and things had changed for him. For better or worse, his life had changed. However, more importantly, he had changed. He knew where his life's blood flowed and it was to Morgan. His desire was only for her.

"Lady Elizabeth, I have a wife, and it's only her to whom I wish to return. Please, do not do this on my account. You're a beautiful, young woman. And there will be a man privileged enough to have ya, lass, but I'm not that man."

With those words, he turned. Mounting Trojan in one graceful movement, he unsheathed his sword and held it high, shouting to his troops with all the authority he controlled. "Men, for king, for country, let us be away! The sooner we leave, the sooner we return to those who bring us home again!"

They were off like thunder, moving through the courtyard and out past the gates.

For king, for country, to war.

End Part I
###

About The Author

Ranay James moved to a small farm in East Texas along with her husband and two dogs after walking away from the fast-paced corporate life in 2012.

Ranay graduated from college majoring in accounting and finance with a minor in business management and law. This is very concrete subject matter as a major. Becoming a romance writer seems a most unlikely path for a woman who spent most of her career managing people and operational practices within the corporate environment.

It all began in 2004 on New Year's Day. Having made a list of things that she wanted to accomplish for the year, she added some items to that list that would push her skill set, and take her out of her comfort zone. Learning to speak Spanish and write a novel were the two items that she felt would stretch her abilities the most, having no prior training in either. Later that day, Ranay sat down at her computer. Looking at that blank Word document, she simply wrote the first thing that came into her mind.

"What were you thinking?" she wrote, having remembered the line from a dream she had in a hotel room in Houston, Texas in 2002. Several chapters in, Ranay found her voice as the story began to form. It poured out from a place that she never knew existed. Ranay began to write that day in 2004 and simply never stopped.

With twelve published works to her name, and nine more completed awaiting publication, Ranay has found a new passion—the love of storytelling and sharing her characters with the world.

Connect with the Author

Please visit Ranay James on Facebook:
http://www.facebook.com/pages/Ranay-James/441095109282762

Join The James Gang Newsletter
http://ow.ly/tTIqH

Twitter
https://twitter.com/ranayjames

Email Me
Info@ranayjames.com

Other Series By Ranay James

Series by Ranay James available in e-book format at all major retailers through the following website:

WWW.booklaunch.io/ranayjames

The McKinnon Legends A Time Travel Series
The McKinnon American Men A Romantic Suspense Series
Vampires Of Nirvana is a ten part series that with each book will leave you begging for more. If you love the McKinnons, then you are going to love the royal family of Nirvana.

Print Editions Available:

Vampires of Nirvana:Book 1- Never Kiss Me Goodbye
Vampires of Nirvana: Book 2 - Point of No Return
The McKinnon The Beginning: Book One Part 1
The McKinnon The Beginning: Book One Part 2
Unfinished Business: Book Two Part 1
Unfinished Business: Book Two Part 2

Large Print Editions:
The McKinnon The Beginning: Book One Part 1
Vampires of Nirvana Book 1 - Never Kiss Me Goodbye

Audiobook Editions:
Audiobooks available at Audiobooks.com and
Audible.com